Off
My
Leash

Meg,

Thanks for everything.

"Jessie" would have

liked you!

X. Céanne

Off My Leash

A Dog's Memoir

by

Diane Badger

TATE PUBLISHING
AND ENTERPRISES, LLC

Published by Tate Publishing & Enterprises, LLC
127 E. Trade Center Terrace | Mustang, Oklahoma 73064 USA
1.888.361.9473 | www.tatepublishing.com

Tate Publishing is committed to excellence in the publishing industry. The company reflects the philosophy established by the founders, based on Psalm 68:11,
"The Lord gave the word and great was the company of those who published it."

Published in the United States of America

ISBN: 978-1-63268-115-7
Pets / Dogs / General
14.06.18

In loving memory of Jessie 1992–2007

Contents

Introduction

We treat our dogs as if they were 'almost human'; that is why they really become 'almost human' in the end.

—C. S. Lewis

In 2007, our wonderful dog of fifteen years passed away. We'd watched helplessly as Jessie's health declined and the quality of her life diminished—all things we expected of an aging dog. During the final week of her life, I spent most of my waking moments savoring our fleeting time together. I was taken by the expressive gaze of her lovely soulful eyes, and I had a sense that somewhere in that mind of hers, the wheels were still turning and she had her own story to tell if she could. At the moment of her passing, I had a strong feeling that something meaningful happened as her soul left her body. Having nothing to substantiate that possibility, I offer this book in the spirit of hope for things we can't see.

Purely fantasy, the following story is a fictional account of what Jessie might have been thinking during those final days we spent together. The entire narrative is her epic mind-journey as she looks back on her past. Ultimately she reaches her own conclusions about the meaning of her life and death.

Part 1

Her face, once velvety red, is now peppered in mostly white—her trophy for a life well lived. Nobody knows for sure what goes on in the mind of a dog at a time such as this.

Diamonds in the Rough

A righteous man cares for the needs of his animal, but the kindest acts of the wicked are cruel.

Proverbs 12:10 (NIV)

I was probably born on or about January 1, 1992. At least that was the best estimate my veterinarian Dr. King could give my *forever* family about four months later. I remember that it was really cold during those earliest days of my life, both physically and emotionally. I still remember my birth mom, although mostly from a viewpoint of helplessness and blind trust. I have a vague mental image of what she looked like, yet the details are somewhat sketchy at best. I have no memory of what her name was. Thinking back, I don't believe I ever heard my birth mom addressed verbally on any personal level. From my perspective at the time, she was my only source of warmth and nourishment; but as I look back, clearly she must have felt much more for me and my siblings. I remember she would nervously pace back and forth, at least as far as the short chain she was tethered to would allow. Although sometimes left unleashed, she was never willing to venture too far from her puppies. After each call to guard duty, she'd crawl back to us and squash us to bits as she settled into our crowded cardboard box home located beneath the rickety porch of a neglected old house somewhere in rural northern New England. These earliest of thoughts are as clear as mud though. When I try to think back as far as I can, my mind does form blurry images, yet I can't be sure if they're actual memories. For certain, I can say I loved the warmth my birth mom brought to our dark nest beneath that old house, as that memory *is* clear enough. When she wasn't in our midst, we were always chilled to the bone. Mostly, though, the fuzzy memories I do have of my first few weeks of life don't feel good to remember, and I may have blocked some of the worst of them out. All my life, I've occasionally exhibited sudden terror for no apparent reason. I've often overheard Mom and Dad allude to the probable turmoil of my early life to explain this odd behavior.

I remember them like they happened yesterday, but all these memories took place within a dog's lifetime—my lifetime, to be exact. I just turned fifteen years old. Or, as my veterinarian likes to put it, "…well into her nineties." I've known for a while that I'm dying. Believe me when I say this is harder on my folks than it is on me. We just celebrated Christmas a week ago, and clearly, this isn't how they expected their new year to begin. I can see the anxiety in their expressions, and worrying about Mom and Dad is what's stressing me out, not my departure from this world. I've lived a great dog's life, and my owners have given me a generous amount of liberty and freedom. This has allowed me to satisfy my curiosities about what goes on outside of my own back yard. But I'm tired now and physically impaired enough that this life has nothing left to offer me except frustration that I can't do what I once was able to do and, of course, more pain. I would love to tell them that I'm not fearful, as I can see Mom is clearly afraid for me. As my body gets weaker and my senses, once sharply honed, continue to fade, I instinctively know the time is imminent when release from suffering will come at last. I'm okay though, with giving Mom the additional time she needs to be at peace with her decision to let me go when she feels ready emotionally to deal with it and not a moment sooner. I don't see this as selfishness, though some might. The way I see it, an extra day or two won't make that much difference. She'll know when the time is right. It'll take a long time for Mom to get over the loss of my companionship, if she ever does. Dad's tougher and more resilient, seeing things in black and white like most men, and not prone to melancholy like she is. That's okay, though, as I completely trust in their timing. In the meantime, I'm content to lie here with my head in Mom's lap where she's been holding vigil for days beside me on the floor.

Actually, I'm finding that reflecting on my past life experiences helps to keep my mind preoccupied. I'm amazed at what I've retained in the innermost archives of this weary dog brain of mine. That last gush of early memory flowed out so effortlessly! I think I'll continue down this path of memory lane as long as I'm still lucid and have clarity of recall, since I don't know how much longer I'll have the full use of my mind. No doubt dredging up this historical accounting of my entire fifteen years of life will be fatiguing, but it might help to tire me enough to get a little sleep here and there as I mentally muddle my way through. At the very least, all this reminiscing might give me something else to think about besides this gnawing ache in my gut. Just how I'm going to get back outside to do my *business* later on these useless legs of mine when the inevitable cramps begin again has got me worried. I know Mom and Dad will do their best to carry the sixty-five pounds of dead weight I've become down the ramp and back up again, but it's downright frustrating for me to be of no help in their efforts. And that's another thing—that ramp has been a thorn in my side since Dad built it last fall. For some reason, it freaks me out, and I don't trust it. I've seen other dogs use them, but as for me, I'd prefer the porch steps. But Mom and Dad can be as stubborn as me when they want to be, so they keep insisting that we use the ramp. Usually, I get my way, but I'm in no condition to resist them these days. I'll try not to think about that right now, let myself drift back in time, and maybe I can pick up where I left off earlier…

When I was still a very young puppy, our living quarters beneath the porch with its tattered screen consisted of a space about six feet by eight feet with about eighteen inches of headspace. This would require my birth mom to crouch in order to navigate about when she was with us. We were afforded privacy by a wooden lattice skirt that surrounded most of the porch. I recall that it seemed to be in a serious state of disrepair but intact enough to keep out the bulk of any sunlight or fresh air that might try to creep in. Consequently, our collapsing box bed remained stubbornly damp and not much of a warm haven of rest and coziness. Access to our dingy hovel was provided by a broken section of the latticework skirt on the north side of the house where the sun seldom shown. In a pinch though, entry was possible through the many missing slats that provided holes, just big enough for puppies to squeeze through.

She did occasionally get petted, but my birth mom's people showed her little else in the way of kindness. Her sudden yelping, followed by their taunting dialog and cackling laughter, which we sometimes heard coming from the porch above, gave us reason to believe something of a sadistic nature was going on. Confused and afraid, we would retreat further below deck. That's where she'd soon rejoin us, licking her fresh sores and otherwise not venturing too far from our soggy bed, unless duty called. Whatever my birth mom endured may have been her reason for keeping us out of sight and hopefully out of the minds of her humans. Her efforts to keep us at least minimally contented with the comfort her presence gave when she crawled below deck to join us, worked for a time. As we grew more independent and energetic, however, our secret existence became too much of a challenge for her. And I'm sure, now that I think about it, we must have been a source of considerable worry for her. Some of us puppies were more spirited than others. I was probably the least rambunctious of the litter, and I lacked curiosity. I seldom joined my siblings in their scouting expeditions outside of our dingy compound. A few weeks after our birth, my siblings and I became less dependent on our birth mom and became fewer in number, mysteriously disappearing one at a time.

The barely satisfactory kibble her people sometimes remembered to feed her was the only care her owners provided for my birth mom. They never showed her offspring even a hint of regard or affection once our existence became known. I had no way of knowing our original headcount, and as my litter mates began diminishing in number, I lost count of how many didn't make it back to the den for dinner. Selfishly, I wasn't all that eager for their return since their disappearance meant a better chance for me to nurse. No doubt, I must have been the runt of the litter, and my hunger wasn't always appeased. My lack of early nourishment most probably was the cause of the timid and lethargic nature of my infancy.

It's uncanny that I was never taken as our brood diminished. I suppose this was because I was smaller and able to hide my existence more effectively when the humans were taking a headcount. I've sometimes reflected on this, and I've decided it was because I was predestined to go to the people who eventually became my *forever* family, namely Mom and Dad. Back then, my life vacillated between the utter boredom of our sunless underworld below the decrepit porch, and fear. This was an emotion that was apparently channeled to us through our birth mom. Although we seldom knew or understood what triggered her fears, we were quick to learn and obediently emulated her shaking and panting when she called on us to do so.

The lack of meaningful substance in our usual daily routine was offset by our preoccupation with observing the colorful parade of dubious looking human characters that came regularly to conduct business of a nefarious nature. They came and went at all hours of the day and night. These visitations were brief in nature, and few words were ever exchanged between them and my birth mom's people who lived in the old house above us. It was probably the only thing that kept us from dying of sheer boredom. In almost every case, my siblings—at least what was left of them—would crawl to the edge of the porch and peer out through the holes in the latticework. If it was daylight, their milky blue puppy eyes would be squinting, as they were unaccustomed to the direct sunlight, yet they had a strong urge to satisfy their curiosity. Then they would be frantically nudged back to the deepest recesses of our nest below by our birth mom until the cars and their strange occupants had driven away, and it was deemed safe for us to come out. I suppose, thinking about it now, my birth mom may have been subjected to occasional abuse by some of those people too and was only trying to prevent the same treatment from being foisted on one of us. One of the cars that arrived on occasion had a tendency to backfire, which really scared our litter, and we'd cry out in terror and scramble in all directions till our birth mom would round us up and restore calm. Eventually, the constant droning of engine noise as vehicles traveled up and down the long gravel drive became so commonplace we were able to sleep through most of it.

My birth mom had an incredible ability to recognize most of the many folks who came by. Just to make sure they weren't impostors though, she would sniff at their clothing and hands and never wag her tail, lest she give them the impression of weakness in the chain of security. She was no pushover, and she performed her guard duties well. Only after they passed inspection would she allow them to go on through the doorway into the screened porch. Although it was an infrequent event, she could dazzle us with the level of ferocity she would exhibit should the visitor not be on the guest list, which she always mentally maintained on behalf of her owners!

And so that's some of what I remember of the first few bleak, cold weeks of my life—a period of time Mom and Dad will never know about, and I will forever be unable to share it with them. My people have no idea how many times I would have gladly told them everything about me. At times, I would sit by my folks and hear them responding in anger and sadness over an animal charity's television appeal or while watching an animal rescue show on *Animal Planet*, one of my favorite television channels. It would bring to my mind some of my own experiences that weren't all that different from what they were watching on the television!

I once overheard Mom speak about a strange phenomenon where they say when you're about to die, your whole life flashes before you. Now that I'm a senior at fifteen years of age, I'm experiencing an end of life total recall of my own. Yet I'm unable to communicate all these memories to my folks in a way they could understand. Our primitive communication has worked fine all these years on a mundane level, I suppose, but I would love to have filled in the blanks and shared so many of the details. Then they could at least know the reasons behind my faults and limitations. It wouldn't surprise me though, if it turned out that they know much more about what makes me tick than I've given them credit for. There's a strong psychic bond that I share with my people, and not everything has to be communicated through the spoken word. There's comfort in knowing this.

When I try to think back to my early youth, the facts become clearer after the initial two months of my life. From that point on, I'm able to recall some experiences with such clarity. It's as if they occurred only yesterday...

I don't recall the exact moment I first met Doug, but he knew my birth mom's people, and he was my first human interaction.

Neither one of us knew it at the time, but he was going to play a major role in orchestrating my future destiny. I knew he was named Doug because I overheard him being called by that name. He was probably in his early adulthood, was strikingly tall and thin, towering over most of the other humans. His thick wiry black hair was pulled back into a tangled mass that sat at the nape of his neck. A friendly grin filled with crooked white teeth complimented his caramel-colored face with its smattering of facial hair. A pair of thick black brows framed his soft brown eyes, which gave him a look of a compassionate individual. In the world we were entangled in, someone nice like Doug seemed out of place, so he stood out to me among the other humans. I would later find out his home was the only other residence on our dead end gravel road. I sensed that his shy and awkward relationship toward my birth mom's humans was probably just self-preservation on his part. In taking the position of submission, he was affording them the respect they didn't deserve. Maybe, now that I think about it, he was just trying to keep his enemies close, so he'd know what they were up to. He showed up at the old house at least once a week, on foot and with a six-pack of beer under his arm. Doug had a long sloping stride as he ambulated up the drive toward the house. His face would turn bright red whenever one of the humans spoke to him, especially if it was a female. I wasn't able to understand what they said to Doug, but from the way they spoke teasingly and laughed at his embarrassment as they shoved him around, I sensed he was the brunt of their cruel jokes—yet they seemed happy enough to drink the beer he'd brought. When it was gone and after tiring of poking fun at him, my birth mom's people would retreat back into the old house. I could almost sense the relief Doug must have felt when he was no longer the focus of their malicious attention, and he was finally free to focus his attention on us.

Around our litter, though, Doug was carefree and affectionate, and he seemed to have a genuine concern for our welfare. After making us beg first, he would dig deep into his pocket and pull out a package of cellophane-wrapped cookies. Hearing the crackling of the wrapper, we would go crazy with excitement and anticipation. My birth mom always got a couple of cookies, but Doug would crumble one of them into small crumbs for me and my siblings. In the free-for-all that followed, I was too small and clumsy to get my fair share. Thankfully, Doug noticed that and provided for it by lifting me out of the fray. He'd then feed me from the open palm of his hand the few crumbs he'd held back from the others.

Special attention was something I almost never got and was quite needy for by the time Doug entered my life. Those eyes of his triggered a strange desire within me to bond with him. However, back then I remained reserved and too conflicted to act on my own instincts where people were concerned. He was the only human my birth mom seemed to accept with welcoming uninhibited appreciation. Her tail always wagged eagerly at his approach. Always first taking my cue from my birth mom, I braved his advances as much as I could bear, despite my extreme shyness. Usually, these brief respites from our otherwise rigidly grim existence would be interrupted by the sudden arrival of another car or the raucous voices of my mom's people in the house. Either situation would cause my birth mom to quickly round up her herd of four or three or whatever was left of us and force us reluctantly back to the safety of our damp and stinking den. From that vantage point, we looked through the broken lattice and watched in despair as Doug, taking the car's approach as his cue to leave, awkwardly loped back home, leaving us helpless and alone against forces we had no control over. I had no way of knowing it at the time, but before long, Doug would provide my only lifeline as, unbelievably, things were about to get much worse for me.

I was never to know what sort of activities took place in the dark, enigmatic world inside the house that stood over us. Judging from the clientele and my instinctive sense that something wicked transpired behind those walls, I'm certain now that it must have been exceedingly evil. Being a dog, I would forever be ignorant in matters of human commerce, both legal and illegal. Whatever the nature of the family business conducted by my birth mom's people was, I doubt that the course of history would have changed even if I had known. It's entirely possible, though, that my overcurious siblings may have gotten too close for comfort, snooping where they shouldn't have, and paying a heavy price for their innocent naughtiness. But deep in my heart, I sincerely hope this wasn't the case, and that they've gone off to find *forever* homes of their own. Realistically though, I know the chances of that are slim to none. As for me, I was instinctively more cautious; and if my curiosity was piqued, I always investigated from a vantage point of safety and seclusion. Eventually, all my siblings turned up missing, and only I was left alone with my birth mom. This is most certainly because I kept myself content within the invisible walls of my small universe underneath the porch—an area that had been my home from birth. This ability would serve me well throughout my life.

One terrible night in particular stands out in my memory. As my birth mom and I huddled together for warmth, we were awakened by the sudden roaring of a speeding car on its approach toward the house. This was followed by the screeching of brakes as the car stopped just short of the front steps. It was so close to us that we could feel the heat of the engine radiating from under the hood. The arriving occupant didn't wait for my birth mom's approval when she grudgingly crawled out to do her usual inspection. Her humans quickly ushered the intruder onto the battered old porch and directly into the house, obviously having expected the late arrival. Her guard duties not required, my birth mom was free to scoot back over to me where she settled into our box, and we resumed our fitful sleep. Not long after we were again rudely awakened by the sounds of a nasty argument in the house above us. Although this wasn't necessarily unusual, the arguing we heard on that particular occasion had, in its intensity, a tone unrivaled by any former verbal exchanges of the past. My birth mom began to fret, whined nervously and trembled, though not from the cold this time as her eyes rolled wildly in their sockets. I had a sense she knew from previous experience that the outcome of that night's events wouldn't bode well for us. The arguing continued for what seemed like hours and into the early morning. Finally, we heard the slam of a car door followed by the spray of gravel and screeching as the car peeled out down the driveway. No further sound came from above, and we eventually settled into dreamless, irritable sleep as the sun began its morning ascent on the horizon.

We awoke soon after to another sunny but cold day only to look out from behind the broken lattice slats and see the people who lived in the house quickly packing up their old pickup. I remember the sky was fiercely bright, and an ominous feeling hung in the air, evidenced by a strange scent my developing canine nose was picking up. A sinking sensation of dread clutched at my belly, and we nervously watched the scene unfold from beneath the porch, trying to gauge the significance of it all. Then, after what seemed like hours, our private abode was invaded by the presence of a human hand, its arm stretching menacingly toward us. It was a hand I'll always remember distinctly. It's funny that I can still see and smell that hand clearly in my mind to this very day, fifteen years later. It appeared suddenly, and I watched in horror as my birth mom, unable to escape the grasp of her human captor, was snatched up from my side. She was harnessed to a choke collar and spirited away toward the waiting truck where she fought against her abductor in her unwillingness to separate from me. As she whimpered, attached to the end of the short chain, she was dragged to the truck's tailgate; and along with several pieces of furniture and boxes, she was quickly lifted up and tethered to the inside of the pickup's bed. She was barely able to keep her balance as she was forced to sit upon a precariously unstable grouping of household items and boxes that had been carelessly stowed in the rush.

Horrified, I slunk to the porch's edge to get a better view of the scene as my teeth chattered involuntarily. Seeing my birth mom being treated this way drove me from below deck—a place of safety I would have hated to venture from normally. In spite of my fears, my courage won out that day, and I bravely skittered to the rear of the truck. I barked and cried in despair as I looked up at my birth mom where she teetered unsteadily— tied to what I think was some kind of a rusty bed frame where she tried to maintain her footing on the shaky perch. Standing on my weak puppy hind legs, I clawed at the lowered tailgate in a futile attempt to climb aboard and rescue my mom. I yelped persistently, desperate at my frailty, my anger mounting at her human captors. Seeing my valiant but helpless efforts on her behalf only served to increase my mom's anxiety. Her scolding frenzied bark, ordering me to return to the porch, went ignored by me. If instinct told me anything that day, it was that my birth mom wasn't going to be with me much longer; and her persistent agonized barking would be my last memory of her, although I have dreamed about her often over my lifetime.

The next thing I remember is being grabbed by the scruff of my neck. I clearly identified the hand that grabbed me as being the one that had just recently assaulted my birth mom. As I was hoisted up and manhandled by this human who surprised me from behind, my legs flailed about loosely. I tried without success to bite the hand with my tiny baby teeth but was unable to turn my head from its grip. Delivering a slap to the side of my face, my cruel tormentor carried me back to the porch and held me down with unnecessary brute force, as I was as weak as a newborn back then. Using his free hand, he shackled me to the porch support with the very chain that had held my birth mom, against her will, most of her life. The chain was wrapped around my neck and front quarters in a tangled mass of bondage since I had no collar to attach it to. Now, with me securely out of their way, the humans continued to remove things from the house and threw them into the truck. Incredibly thirsty as I was from all my crying, and heavily restrained, I could just barely reach the icy puddle below the dripping spigot, which had been our only source of water.

The last merciless act of my jailers was their attempt to set the house on fire. As I cowered under the edge of the porch steps, I watched as a strong smelling liquid was poured from a can along the lattice skirting around the house's perimeter, and after setting fire to a rag and throwing the burning torch, the last of these despicable humans jumped into the waiting truck. I watched in disbelief as the pickup tore off scattering snow, mud and loose gravel in its wake and leaving me to burn at the stake. For the next few minutes, I watched and waited in terror as the flames grew and rose from the liquid spill. I could feel the heat of the fire within a few feet of my face, and the odd chemical smells assaulted my sensitive nostrils. I strained with all my might and pulled the short chain taut until it gave no more. What I now believe, but failed to comprehend as a puppy, was that the intention of the humans was to destroy any evidence of their mischief that may have been left behind. What their reasons may have been for including me in the plan of destruction still boggles my mind.

Fortunately for me, I didn't die that day. For whatever reason, the fire died out before it was able to fully engage and do much damage. At the very most, the damage consisted of a black sooty residue on the clapboard siding and a residual burnt wood smell that hung in the air. But from my vantage point, I could see very little consequence to the overall integrity of the house's structure. The trauma of what occurred that day left me wretchedly shaken. The earlier sunshine had long since given way to a raw overcast sky, and as the late afternoon wind kicked up, I shuddered, uncomfortably cold. I laid down in defeat with my chin upon my front paws and kept my eye on the long driveway, hoping my birth mom would somehow escape and come back to me. It grieves me sometimes to remember what sort of people my birth mom had the misfortune of belonging to. Although she no doubt had opportunities to escape before and after her brood was born, she stayed and served her people with stubborn loyalty. Expecting nothing and getting even less than that in return, she chose her tormentors over freedom in the true spirit of dog servitude. For this reason, she stands out as a heroin and a martyr in my eyes. As it is with most dogs, she was able to unconditionally love the human family that fate had dealt her.

Later that day, hours after her people drove off with my birth mom, it began to snow and sleet as evening finally closed in. Eventually, I realized that my mom wasn't going to respond to my cries as she had in the past. I crawled back to my shabby dank sanctuary out of the freezing drizzle and tried to make sense out of what made no sense. There I huddled, alone this time, without my birth mom's warmth, in the empty box home, which by now had seen better days. It still had her smell, but that was little solace. By the next day, the sunshine had returned, and I woke with my usual hunger. As I squirmed in my box bed in search of my mom's nourishment and warmth, my hopes were dashed as I awoke fully and remembered all that had taken place the day before. My hunger grew by the minute, and, being at least partially weaned, I remembered suddenly that I was sitting on a bone yard of buried meat scraps and bones, courtesy of my birth mom's resourcefulness. These were the leftovers from her people's meals that she'd scavenged surreptitiously from a garbage pit on the side of the house that was burned weekly. She'd wisely buried those provisions, remembering the lean times when they would forget to feed her the meager ration of dry dog kibble they sometimes gave her. I had the good fortune to be chained within reach of some of those burial sites. Even now, I still get shivers of delight when I smell that wonderful fetid odor of rancid, decaying marrow that only a dog could love. Although my rations are far more generous these days, I've never been able to shake the habit of burying food treasures. I suppose this is due to my survival instincts, made sharper because of my humble beginnings. Back then though, there wasn't much left of the marrow in those old filthy bones, but they were one step away from eating actual dirt, which would have been my next option.

This was my dismal existence for the next few days as I lay sprawled out under the edge of the porch with my chin resting on a broken slat in the lattice. In that position, I kept my daily watch as I looked out upon my world in a weakened state of inertia. Day after endless day, I searched the bleak horizon for signs of my birth mom. Instead of experiencing the joy of her returning to me, I only experienced the boredom of watching a relentless sun come up on my left, take what seemed like eternity to inch its way across the sky to my right where, predictably, it sank back down toward the earth. There it set on a vast wasteland of leafless trees upon which the tired old house sat. Then, practically snow blind, I would eventually go to sleep and dream my empty puppy dreams, which were the result of my empty puppy life.

Weakened to the point of listlessness, I remained in a hopeless state of inactivity until one morning, after a sleepless night of sadness and hunger, I was awakened by the crunching of human footsteps in the snow. My first emotion upon hearing them was fear. In my muddled thoughts, it had occurred to me that my birth mom's people might be coming back to finish me off. Forcing myself to look yet too weak to make a fast retreat under the porch, I lifted my heavy eyelids, and there standing before me was Doug with a six-pack of beer under his arm. Looking puzzled at first, he slowly began to assess the scene before him. As for me, I stared up at him in a daze. I was confused and without my mom to cue me, not sure how to react to him. The usually docile Doug was livid, seeing me filthy and starving. The black residue on the clapboards and porch steps was more than enough evidence to convince him that there'd been an obvious diabolical plot to destroy me along with the house. Doug didn't call the authorities though, as I guess he feared that his presence there might cause the authorities to believe he was implicated in the crime. I don't hold this against him, as his actions following his discovery of me were commendable.

After his initial shock over the scene before him, Doug sat beside me on the porch where he worked to untangle the frozen chains that were wrapped around me. I relaxed, knowing that he was my only hope, as he tried to make sense of the series of loops and knots that seemed to have no rhyme or reason. Giving up, he ran home with his usual long clumsy gait and returned minutes later in an old car and a pair of bolt cutters, which he used to release me from my prison of the last few days and the den of horrors that had been my home for most of my barely three months of life.

My legs were wobbly from lack of exercise because of my birth mom's reluctance to allow me to wander too far from her. This weakness was exacerbated by several days of inactivity during my chained captivity. I was unable to support my own weight, so Doug carefully lifted me into the back seat of the car and covered me with a mildewed blanket, which he'd retrieved from the trunk. It smelled wonderful to me. Even now, the memory of my first sweet taste of human kindness and compassion will always return to me when I smell anything moldy or musty. As Doug drove away, I guess I knew that the life I had shared with my birth mom was probably over. I have to confess here that I've secretly harbored a belief that my birth mom and I would meet again—maybe in a special heavenly place reserved for all the dogs who ever lived and especially those that had some bad breaks in this earthly life and have gone on to a better one. This hasn't kept me from missing her though. I have sometimes mused on the brief and bittersweet time we had together, although the pain of separation has faded.

Strangely, during the last few years of my life, I find that I've been dreaming about my birth mom a lot; and lately, it's been occurring even more frequently. In my dream, I usually spot her somewhere on a rolling hillside. She never sees me in return, it's just me seeing her, and it's frustrating when I'm not able to communicate with her or get her attention. There is a bit of comfort though in just watching her and checking out all the details about her that I never bothered to take note of when I was a puppy. I'm amazed at how much I resemble her in so many ways. Yet certainly some of my features were obviously acquired from my birth dad whom I never knew. One feature that does stand out in my memory of my birth mom is her beautiful sad eyes. In one of my dreams, I thought she saw and recognized me; but as she ran toward me, she went right past, almost brushing my shoulder as she flew by. Her familiar scent hung in the air long after she ran past me but eventually dissipated. By the time I woke up, it was gone. Sometimes when I go to bed, I try to think about my birth mom because that usually helps bring on those dreams about her.

Baby Steps

Friendship is born at that moment when one person says
to another, "What! You too? I thought I was the only one."

—C. S. Lewis

I was about three months of age when I went to live with Doug.
After examining my injuries closely and taking my weakness into
account, he made an uneducated guess that my prognosis was
good. Then and there Doug determined to nurse me to good
health in time for his planned departure for a place he called
Florida. My failure to thrive thus far had set me behind in much
of my development, and I had some serious catching up to do.
I often look back on this period of rest and recuperation with
pangs of yearning.

Due to the dysfunctional nature of my early home life, I wasn't
properly weaned, and I was far overdue for this. My birth mom
had continued to allow me to nurse much longer than what would
be deemed normal, having no other recourse to provide for my
nourishment. Toward the end of our life together, she'd been more
reluctant to let me nurse and was drying up anyway. What little
mother's milk she produced failed to satisfy me. As I consider this
now, I can only speculate that her lack of food and insufficient
drinking water left her with barely enough nourishment to
sustain herself. Because I was clearly unaccustomed to only solid
food, Doug prepared a mashed blend of canned food and milk
for me, and I enjoyed it immensely. Since those canned foods

were probably meant only for human consumption, I sometimes had tummy distress during that time. Soon after, Doug dispensed with the special food preparation and began feeding me right from the can, dropping spoonfuls onto a paper plate on the couch in front of me. I would sit alongside him as we ate. He watched the TV while I watched the can we ate from to be sure I got my fair share. He shared everything he had with me including his plentiful supply of snacks. I remember the peanut butter sandwich cookies that came in little six packs, like the ones he used to bring to our hungry brood back at the old house. He would eat five of them and then give me one, because I was smaller. This was probably the beginning of my lifelong fondness for anything with peanut butter. In fact, peanut butter would one day be the vehicle upon which my prescription pills would ride as they traveled down my esophagus. Back then at Doug's, when it came to food, it was share and share alike. He kept a bucket of water always at my disposal, and I drank liberally—suffering initially from a tremendous thirst that was eventually quenched after a few days. I didn't miss my dependence on the dripping spigot, which had barely been sufficient during my last few days at the old house, unless the drip froze, in which case there was always melting snow.

Doing my *business* wherever it suited me was a problem at first. Since I had never before been inside a human's house, my inability to distinguish between the outdoors and the living quarters of Doug's home was a challenge for him. Initially, he thought the solution was to keep me confined in the tiny galley kitchen at night, blocking the entrance into the other parts of the house. A normal dog would be instinctively unwilling to foul his or her own sleeping and eating area. In most cases, this ploy would have been a successful house-training tool. However, this tactic did not work for me since the unusual constraints of my under-the-porch home during my formative infancy didn't allow for a separate waste area. Because of this, *going* in my living space wasn't as abhorrent to me as it should have been. Perhaps Doug sensed this because he began taking me outside hourly. I quickly found that I actually preferred relieving myself outside—and it seemed more natural to me anyway. As a result of his diligence, I eagerly took to being house-trained. I patiently waited until Doug, an early riser, got up each morning to escort me to the taller weedy grasses, still snow-covered, on the outer edge of the yard. Leading me on a rope leash, he taught me to keep the lawn clean by restricting my ability to *go* where it might likely be stepped upon. I didn't mind using the taller grasses along the lawn's outer perimeter, and in fact, I appreciated the privacy it afforded me too.

I particularly remember how beautiful the yard was at Doug's. It was in stark contrast to the muddy slush and gravelly terrain of my former home, which had been strewn with discarded cigarettes, dog scat, trash, and other various forms of debris and disorder. Within a week, I knew what was expected of me; and apart from an occasional mishap, depending on the meal I'd consumed the night before, I almost always was able to control my urges. I looked forward to the praise Doug liberally gave me for my efforts. After that time, I was given clearance to bunk in with this new person of mine, where I took up more than my share of his incredibly comfortable bed and its wonderfully aromatic musty blanket.

At Doug's place, the condition of the inside of his house was somewhat disordered and relaxed. With the limited experience I had, I don't know how I was able to make that distinction. I'm not judging; I'm only making an observation as I try to remember exactly what it looked like at Doug's. His clothing was strewn about covering every bit of floor space. His bed was always unmade, and trash littered every surface, seldom finding its way to the barrel at the kitchen door. In spite of the chaos, his home was far and away superior to the abysmal trappings I was used to under the porch of the old house, so I wasn't terribly squeamish about the mess. On the contrary, I took great pleasure in the aroma of not-so-fresh food coming from inside the empty cans and dirty dishes that lay about the kitchen. One day when I was left alone in the house, I tried to lick out one of the discarded empty cans and cut my tongue. I remember it stung for days every time I ate after that. I remember too that I loved the strong smell of sweat on his dirty laundry, and I took to lying on the piles of it he left here and there.

Once I was house-trained, he allowed me to have full freedom of expression. Running and barking inside the house were always tolerated and even encouraged by Doug, who appeared to thrive on this type of chaotic atmosphere. Laughing, he would chase me from room to room; and then it was my turn to chase him while I did the laughing—or barking, as I couldn't really laugh! Slowly but surely, Doug and I were being drawn out of our former insecurities and shyness. I gradually became accustomed to making myself as comfortable as I could wherever it suited me. As I saw it, Doug and I were equals. We ate identical meals, and we shared the same bed. What was his was mine. I totally enjoyed the liberties afforded to me after the three months of house arrest at my former home. I was pretty innocent and naïve then, but I realize now that Doug was a peculiar individual, very childlike and quirky. I suppose this was the reason he seemed to have no meaningful friendships with other humans but easily connected with dogs, as we tend to be nonjudgmental about people. In hindsight, I believe Doug and I were drawn together because we were both underdogs living in a world that could be harsh and unjust if you didn't fit in to what society considered the norm. He taught me most of what I know about being eccentric— something I'm often accused of being to this very day.

My first spring was fast approaching at that time, and soon patches of green were showing as the snow began to melt on the lawn of Doug's house. Green grass was a new and refreshing sight as I had only seen snow and icy mud at the old house. The days were becoming longer and warmer too, and the floral overtones and damp freshness of the air stung my nostrils and stirred my inner senses, somehow making me melancholy for something I couldn't quite grasp. I can't for the life of me imagine how that was possible considering that, up to that time, I'd never before experienced anything worthy of causing this stirring within me. Yet at those times, I'd think about my birth mom and how she had loved me but tried and failed to protect me. I wondered where she was and hoped she was enjoying the smell of the air too.

Until my boundaries were established, Doug led me about with a rope when we were outdoors, but he did give me plenty of opportunity to explore. He always kept the leash slack, so I didn't feel compelled to strain against it. I wanted to smell everything I saw; every new thing I encountered was investigated by me as my inventory of sensory connections was rapidly increasing. Far from being the fully developed and finely sharpened tools they would eventually become, my senses at that time were probably already superior to most humans. The trees were beginning to bud and were starting to offer some degree of shade, which I fully appreciated. All the time I'd spent beneath the porch of my birth mom's house had rendered me ultra-sensitive to sunlight. This condition became less pronounced as my exposure to the direct rays of the sun was lengthened gradually each day. Over the years, however, I have preferred to be out of the sunshine and in the shade.

Now, at Doug's place, I was undeterred by the short chain that once held me back or the constant corralling of my birth mom to the safety of our underground lair, and I was free to exercise under Doug's supervision. I became largely fixated on my legs that were markedly weakened by the inactivity of my first twelve weeks of life. They began to get noticeably stronger as a result of Doug's coaching. I was amazed at how they could propel me from place to place in rapid flight, leaving me hot and panting. Then I'd lie in a pile of snow that had yet to melt in spite of the warming days of spring. I would endeavor to practice daily, at the encouragement of Doug, running back and forth through the grass and leftover snow at lightning speed till all traces of my former weakness disappeared.

As the days passed, Doug spent most of his time sorting through his vast array of belongings and began to pack his car in preparation for our trip to the Florida place he often spoke to me about. He told me he had family there, and that he needed to get away where it was warm to make a fresh start. He also said something about running out of funds, and that we'd have to make our move soon. It was really all a jumble of explanations. I remember only certain words, but I've managed to piece them together when I've sometimes reflected on my early past. Because I didn't really understand him at the time, I showed him in the best way I could that none of this mattered to me as long as we were together, and that I adored him immensely. Anticipating the arrival of the house's owner, a person he called his landlady, to inspect the house before our departure, Doug spent most of the week clearing away the winter's debris along with packing and loading the car. Meanwhile, during the day, I was kept tied by the rope to a shade tree that grew alongside the woods so that I wouldn't get in the way of progress, and I was finally allowed to go inside late each afternoon for supper.

On our final night there, when I was allowed to come in that evening for dinner, I noticed that Doug's house was empty of his belongings, and all trash and disorder had been cleared away. To my disappointment, the interior of the house was free of the pungent sweat smell I'd grown accustomed to and loved. The new fragrance had an artificial pine scent that only slightly resembled that of the woods surrounding the house, and it stung my sinuses. Perhaps in time, I would have gotten used to the new aroma, but my first impulse was to sulk and search unsuccessfully for a pile of dirty laundry to plunk down onto. The clean, crisp barrenness seemed odd to me. Only the furniture remained. I found myself growing nervous again after three glorious weeks of freedom from worry and letting my guard down. That night, we shared a couple of cans of corned beef hash. Doug stared blankly at the vacant space where the TV once sat as he ate and I, as usual, watched the can. For once, the animated and clownish antics he was known for were given over to a quietness that was uncharacteristic of him. Lost in his thoughts, he ignored my sulkiness. Desperate for normalcy, I attempted to engage him in a game of Tag, but I was ignored. We went to bed early, and I was disappointed to find that the mildewed blanket had been washed of the wonderful scent that I loved.

Early the next morning, the woman he'd been expecting arrived for the house inspection. She had a kind face, but I remained reserved and didn't approach her when she bent over and extended her arms to me. I remembered the way Doug responded to the women at the old house and suspected they weren't to be trusted as a species. I was tied by my rope to the front porch and told to wait outside. Within a short time, they both emerged; and the woman retrieved a notebook from her car and handed Doug a small piece of paper, which I guess must have been the funds needed to pay for our road trip to Florida. Suddenly, as if just remembering something she almost forgot, she reached back into her car and brought out a paper bag. From where I sat, it smelled wonderful. Since I hadn't been fed, I hoped it was for me. Before I had the chance to pull away, she managed to pet the top of my head as she was leaving.

With nothing left to be done, it was time for us to leave for Florida. Doug led me to the outer edge of the lawn for what would be my last opportunity to *go* for a while. Had I fully understood the finality of the circumstance at the time, that I was never to return to this place, which had come to mean so much to me, I would have taken along the few toys I'd acquired during my stay. They weren't much, but they were my first toys, and they meant a lot to me. There was a throwing stick that

Doug had painstakingly cleaned all the bark off of with his Swiss army knife (until it was rendered free of its potential to irritate my tender baby gums and teeth).

I also had a plastic pink football he'd gotten me on one of his trips to town, along with a fake plastic bone that squeaked when I bit it—I'd hidden that behind the stone wall. I've often thought back and wondered why Doug didn't bother to bring my toys along that day if we weren't coming back. Yet he did remember to bring all of his own belongings. This would have been a red flag for me later in my more mature years but not back then when I was so naïve and trusting of my newfound friend. In my eyes, Doug could do no wrong, and I felt only love and complete reliance upon his care and wisdom on our behalf. When the time came to leave, Doug threw the bag and his battered backpack into the rear seat of his overloaded rusty old car. I had no idea what to expect, but in the spirit of blind trust, I readily followed him with an open and curious mind, eager to see what Doug had planned for us.

Florida or Bust

I trust that everything happens for a reason, even when we're not wise enough to see it.

—Oprah

Initially, the trip went well. I lay sprawled out in the back seat and balanced myself upon the mountain of stuff that represented all of Doug's worldly possessions. I was delighted to find that they smelled strongly of his sweat. As I rested atop this platform, I was entertained by the sound of his voice as he sang in a shrill falsetto way along with a song being played on the radio. This was something he'd often done back at his house, and I'd come to enjoy the sound of it. As we sped along the roadway, I was totally amazed at the world that spun by me. I think what surprised me the most was how big the world was and how limited my earlier perception of it had been. From behind the wheel, Doug beckoned me to climb forward. Obediently, I joined him in the front seat and harmonized with his singing even though I was unfamiliar with the lyrics. A couple of times, Doug even opened my window, and I stuck my head out and let the wind slap my ears against the sides of my face. I figured out that if I opened my mouth with my head turned just a little at a certain angle, the wind would grab my tongue and plaster it to the side of my cheek, and it would stay there until I turned my head back slightly enough to enable me to pull it back into my mouth. I also discovered that the wind could be caught in my cheeks, and by doing so, it would expose all my teeth and gums. This provided considerable entertainment for me, especially when I saw how hideous it made me look in the side mirror.

It wasn't long though before Doug got cold and shut my window. The morning chill of that early spring day felt wonderful to me as I was still wearing most of my winter coat. However Doug, having shed his coat for the car ride, wasn't so cozy. He turned the car's heater on a high setting, and I had to endure a steady blast of unnatural warmth from the heating vents. No matter where I moved, I couldn't escape the hot air. I looked at Doug, hoping he'd take the hint and turn it off, but he ignored me. Returning to the backseat, I managed to dig out a space within the heap of Doug's clothing, which enabled me to escape the jets of overheated air that came from the dashboard in front. Within minutes, I felt cooler and rested in a sort of twilight sleep, just barely conscious, and listened to the distant sound of Doug's singing, which was now somewhat more subdued than earlier.

After a while, I realized I was ravenously hungry. I hadn't eaten a meal since the two cans of corned beef hash that we'd shared the night before. It didn't take long for me to find the bag Doug's landlady had given him earlier that morning. I literally ransacked the bag once I discovered it contained a meatloaf sandwich. I quickly devoured it, not bothering to do much chewing, and I left the bread and lettuce rejected and mangled. Although the meatloaf more than satisfied my appetite, I soon became bored; and just for something to do, I began rooting around and located the snacks Doug brought along for the ride. I searched through this stash looking for a package of the peanut butter cream filled cookies I loved so much. Furtively, I glanced at the back of Doug's head periodically to be sure he wasn't watching me in the rear view mirror. Unable to find the cookies, I attempted to open a bag of potato chips, which were not a favorite of mine, but it was the challenge that drew my interest. The cellophane bag was full of air and proved almost impossible to open in spite of my efforts.

When the bag suddenly did burst at its seam, a sea of crumbled chips spilled out and littered the back seat. I scrambled to devour as many as I could in an attempt to keep Doug from finding out, but I was too full from the meatloaf to eat very many of them. The chips that I couldn't eat eventually found their way into every crack and crevasse of Doug's belongings as they filtered down from the vibrations of the vehicle.

Shortly after my feeding frenzy, I became dizzy and nauseated. For what seemed like eternity, I tried unsuccessfully to get Doug's attention. I whimpered in my distress as I darted from one side to the other and gasped unsuccessfully for fresh air through the closed windows. Meanwhile, Doug was obviously lost in thought because he ignored my cries for help. In my unwillingness to soil myself, I held on as long as my barely disciplined puppy self could. Eventually though, the nausea and cramping became so bad I lost control. This required an unplanned pit stop because it wasn't long before the evidence of my offense made its way through the car's air current into the front seat compartment. I won't go into all the details here, but after Doug finished cleaning up the car and discarded some of the worldly possessions that I helped liberate him from, we got back on the road. Although I did get the silent treatment for a while, he didn't stay mad for long and eventually invited me back into the front seat beside him. With his arm around my shoulder and me pressed up against him, we were best traveling buddies again, although we were no longer in the mood to sing. One good thing that came about from my sickness was that Doug had no choice but to keep both windows wide open for quite a while to dispel the residual scent of my illness. Knowing from experience that this reprieve was just temporary, I gulped all the air my tiny lungs could take in while I had the chance.

Just when I was finally beginning to cool down, Doug once again shut the windows tight, sealing us into an oppressively airtight chamber. The heat upon the old vinyl car seats generated a petroleum smell that nauseated me. The brightness of the sunlight that streamed into the vehicle hurt my light-sensitive eyes, and I almost couldn't bear to keep them open. Also, being intensely thirsty, I realized that Doug had forgotten to give me water. I lay stretched out on the front seat feeling parched, my aching head on Doug's lap. I daydreamed about my water bucket back at his place and wished we had remembered to bring it along. When we did finally stop at a rest area, I leapt out of the car before Doug could stop me and joined a fellow traveling dog as he slurped water from his bowl. He seemed to take no notice of me as my tongue lapped thirstily from his bowl of ice cold water. He was a mountainous black Lab whose folks were parked beside us. They called him Smitty. Apparently, Smitty the Lab and his folks didn't mind my eagerness to share their dog's water without having been invited first. This was good because I fought against Doug's futile attempt to pull me away from the bowl until my intense thirst was fully satisfied. Doug was embarrassed and extended an apology to Smitty's people who offered us a couple of extra bottles of water for the road. I would have gladly accepted their offer but was unable to vocalize this. Doug, being fiercely independent, refused and took an empty plastic milk jug out of the trunk to fill at the building's spigot. After returning from the vending area with snacks, Doug offered me a peanut butter cream filled cookie, but, for once, I wasn't interested in food. By then I had a bad case of motion sickness and a seriously upset stomach. A side trip to the dog walking area helped, although by then, I was an unenthusiastic traveler. My head and tail hung low as I reluctantly followed Doug back to his car where I turned and looked back at Smitty and his people. I implored them, with my sad eyes, to save me. When they didn't, I was led away, like a lamb to the slaughter, and placed back on the seat beside Doug. From that moment, I proceeded to shake as I fought off my continued car sickness.

The high spirits I began the trip with were now clearly gone, replaced by a feeling of entrapment, and soon I was beginning to experience full-blown claustrophobia. It sort of came on suddenly. The sensation was similar to when I'd been chained to the porch support as the fire burned back at the old house. I kept trying to lower myself onto Doug's side of the floor at his feet where it seemed cooler and safer, only to be pulled back up by him off the pedals, by the scruff of my neck. Taking this as rejection and being the willful puppy I still was, I wasn't about to give up. It became a war of wills as Doug did his best to be patient with me yet I could tell that we were losing our grip on the friendship we'd once shared. His resolve not to get too mad at me was being seriously tested, and after a while, he pulled over to the side of the road and tied me with the rope, then tied the other end to the inside armrest of the passenger's side. This made the rope just short enough to prevent me from reaching his side of the car. However, he did leave enough slack to allow me to settle down on the floor of the passenger's side, which I finally resigned myself to do. There, I found that Doug had left a plastic bowl with some water for me. Although it was now lukewarm from the car's heater, it did a lot to restore my calm.

Our relationship had become somewhat strained during those last hours of our short car trip, so we settled into a quiet tolerance of one another. By then we had lost our initial spirit of madcap travel adventure. I know now that I didn't live up to my end of whatever it was he'd bargained for. The whole concept of the trip to Florida, which once had seemed like a wonderful and mysterious escapade, ceased to be exciting to me. It had become tiresome and boring, and I longed for a patch of grass to run on, and I sulked as I suddenly remembered the toys we'd left behind too. Doug's moodiness and inability to realize I had reached my limit of traveling tolerance was getting on my nerves too. I glanced over at his profile as he drove and noticed the twitch in his tightened jaw. The perpetual friendly grin I had come to love had given way to a stern line of thin lips slashed across the lower half of his face. His black brows were drawn together, giving him the appearance of having nervous tension uncharacteristic of the Doug I thought I knew. I guessed I was to blame for the unhappiness the *new* Doug was experiencing, but I had my own problems, so I really didn't care. And I didn't know where or what Florida was, but I desperately hoped we'd be getting there soon as I couldn't take much more of the misery I was feeling.

As fate would have it, I wasn't destined to be a Florida dog. Not long after our last pit stop, the car began to sputter and smoke as it traveled. This seemed to be of grave concern to Doug. He told me that we would be stopping as soon as we reached what he called Massachusetts, so he could try to fix it. I didn't fully comprehend the implications of this but was secretly relieved when the car limped onto an exit ramp and a mile or so later, coughed its way to a complete stop on the side of a busy street in the center of a town. Untying me from the door's armrest, Doug released me, so I could get out and breathe in some cool, fresh air. After I'd relieved myself behind some tall weeds in the back of an alley between buildings, I began to explore the strange and new surroundings I found myself in the midst of. I sniffed everything I could and at the same time tried to stay out of Doug's radar since I wasn't anxious to get back in the car any time soon if I could help it. Doug seemed distracted anyway and was fully preoccupied with the repairs he was attempting under the hood of his wreck.

Since he didn't appear to be concerned with my whereabouts, I took advantage of the freedom I temporarily had from the lull in our not-so-smooth journey. I felt the need to put some space between me and Doug…for a while anyway, so I wandered away for several blocks. Cars and trucks whizzed by, and there were tall buildings and stores all around me. I know what they are now, but at the time, these massive structures were a very strange sight for me. I tried to find a space below them that I could crawl into and watch from a more secretive vantage point, but none of the structures had such a space. There were people too, and they were of a variety I wasn't accustomed to, nicer than the sort of thugs and scoundrels I'd seen back at the old place. I had no reference point with which to gauge it, but I had a sense, or maybe it was a smell, that I was perfectly safe around these particular humans. Without my birth mom to prompt me one way or the other as to how to react to them, I bashfully allowed some of them to stroke my head or scratch my ears. A few smiled at me or spoke in gentle tones. Their friendly intentions were at times misunderstood especially if it was a woman's voice, and I sometimes backed away, alarmed at the sudden movements toward me. They were probably good folks, but my limited experience had taught me that there were good humans and there were bad humans, and I didn't know the difference.

At that point in my life, Doug had been my only positive encounter with humans, and even that relationship was proving to be fragile at best. Since my friendship with Doug was seriously unraveling, I wasn't feeling so positive about it anymore. Looking back, I believe I was so fed up at that moment that if I'd had the courage and hadn't been so dependent still, maybe I would have gone off on my own. I was determined not to get back in that car again. But then, dogs will be dogs; and even though our humans disappoint us at times, we have a difficult time separating ourselves from them once the bond has been established. I loved Doug back then, and I began to feel lonely for him as I wandered through the town that day. I started weaving my way along the busy main street sidewalk, following my scent and markings back to Doug. As I walked, I imagined us going back to the carefree life we had at Doug's place. I knew he was probably feeling the same way as I felt, and I was eager to find the car, so we could get back home in time for his favorite television show.

As I walked, I must have stepped out in traffic a couple of times because the squeal of brakes and honking of car horns got

Doug's attention. With a weary look of frustration, he flung his toolbox into the trunk of his car, slammed the hood shut, and tied the makeshift leash around my neck. I could tell by the strained look in his eyes that he wasn't as happy to see me as I was to see him. He briskly walked with me along the storefronts and didn't allow me to stop and sniff things along the way as he might have done back at his place. Suddenly, he stopped in front of an eating establishment located within a busy block. I knew it had to do with food because of the odor that came from the door when it was opened. Doug began tying me to a street signpost just outside of the diner, which terrified me. I was beginning to smell the faint odor of burning, and I associated it with imprisonment, fire, and abandonment, and I began to whimper and shake uncontrollably. Not understanding, Doug became clearly annoyed with me and began to chew me out. That didn't work either and only caused the people walking by to scowl at his treatment of me. He tried comforting me next, to appease the watchful crowd that had begun to gather.

All this was a waste of time. When my fear instinct is triggered, I see in tunnel vision, and I don't hear or recognize anyone's presence beside me. No amount of reassurance will draw me out of a panicked state, and I begin to pant uncontrollably with my tongue hanging out of my gaping mouth and my eyes wide and unseeing. When I get like this, it's best to leave me alone; and when the time is right, my composure will be restored on its own. It was my good fortune that nobody intervened on my behalf that day. To have done so might have changed the course of history and prevented me from ever meeting my *forever* family, but at the time, I didn't see it that way. Leaving me tied up, the fuming Doug retreated behind the door of the diner. The crowd slowly disbursed, shaking their heads and giving me piteous looks over their shoulders as they reluctantly walked away. Restrained by my short tether, I soon got tired of sitting up. Lying down on the pavement, I eventually stopped shaking and drifted off to sleep.

The next memory I have of that day is Doug kneeling beside me with an odd sort of guilty look on his face as he untied my rope and handed me over to a stranger. He was an older man with steel blue eyes, a tanned face, and a smile that revealed a shining row of pure white teeth. Below his large nose was a gray mustache and several colorful tattoos, which covered most of his neck and arms. He was wearing a baseball cap over a head full of oily gray hair. His breath smelled strongly of tobacco and meat with minty overtones. The man's sweat had an odd but pleasant combination of scents. It fell far short of the odor of sweat that was a smell peculiar only to *my* Doug and that I'd grown to love. The man seemed friendly enough, but for the life of me, I didn't understand why we were being introduced. I was annoyed by his presence, and I was anxious to be alone with Doug, so we could go home. For some reason, I believed we had made a psychic agreement to end our trip and return. They had a brief exchange of words, which clearly pertained to me and my wellbeing; and the man gave Doug some greenish paper, which I now know is money. The man then pointed to an area across the street, and suddenly, my soul mate and mentor of the last three weeks ran back to his car, with me watching intently, and retrieved some of his things. I was shocked to see Doug run to a bus stop across the road about a block away, ignoring my desperate barks that pleaded for him to come back. When I last saw him, he was boarding a bus that had pulled up to the stop, with his old battered backpack, leaving me and his wreck of a car behind. I'm not sure if this really happened or if I just want to believe it did, but I think Doug looked back and waved to me. I didn't understand why I wasn't going with him, and I frantically searched my young mind for an explanation. At the time, I probably thought he'd merely forgotten to come back and retrieve me from this stranger in whose possession I now was. Frantically, I barked, "Doug! Doug!" but it was no use. The bus pulled away from the curb and drove off, leaving a cloud of stinking exhaust in its wake.

This concluded my relationship with Doug. I have never fully understood why Doug abandoned me so easily. I know we could have made it work out between us. It hurt me a lot at the time, but sometimes breakups turn out to be blessings in disguise. Doug really had no clear direction for his own life back then, and I would most certainly have been a considerable burden. Knowing what I know now about proper pet maintenance, it seems obvious Doug was seriously unprepared when he'd taken me in just three weeks earlier. At first his heart was in the right place, but I guess he had what my *forever* Mom calls "commitment issues." His willingness to release me that day to the stranger proved to be for my own good. It was the beginning of a series of events that led to my adoption by Mom and Dad. I do believe, though, that deep down, Doug was a kind soul who did the best he knew how to do for me. I've almost always thought about him with warmth and gratitude and have tried to forget the guilt in his eyes that never looked directly at me when he said good-bye. I hope he found his *forever* family, as I did.

Within the Belly of the Beast

Have enough courage to trust love one more time and always one more time.

—Maya Angelou

Immediately after the bus drove away with Doug, the stranger with the mustache removed the other end of the rope (which by now was damp and badly chewed) from around my neck and tossed it into a trash can nearby. Then, without saying a word, he clutched the loose skin at the back of my neck, the way my birth mom used to do, except she used the gentle pressure of her teeth to do so. He hoisted me up with my head on his shoulder and my bottom quarter resting on his forearm. Carrying me this way, he headed toward the opposite end of the street away from Doug's broken down car. The tip of his mustache tickled my nose. The strangeness of his smooth tanned skin and the smell of his cologne as he spoke in soothing low tones to me sickened me a little. Through no fault of this stranger, my scary past was catching up with me, and I had a brief moment of a very bad memory—a memory I couldn't quite remember the details of. I only know that this memory had been something exceedingly evil.

These snippets of vague, repressed memories of the cruel nature exhibited by the humans I encountered during my early formative weeks of life would continue to torment me over the years. Sometimes they came in the form of nightmares from which my parents had to physically awaken me. The nightmares happened less as I matured, and I've not had one for a very long time now. I no longer fear my past experiences as I once did, and I now know that those memories can no longer hurt me now that I'm safe with my *forever* Mom and Dad.

Imprisoned by the firm muscular grasp of the mustachioed stranger, I was quickly carried along as my eyes darted around for a possible escape route. His hold on me was strong and secure, so I was pretty sure the opportunity would not present itself to break free anyway. I know I must have been confused about Doug's whereabouts at that moment. I don't remember my exact thoughts at the time, but I certainly must have been growing more desperate by the second, because I do remember I had an incredible urge to go find Doug. I recall a primitive sense of regret for not having been nicer to Doug though I was obviously too young for true empathy at that stage of my life. Wiggling around in the stranger's grasp only caused him to squeeze me tighter against his chest. When I continued to resist the pressure of his hold on me, he just shifted my weight to his other arm. In the end, my instinct told me the matter was out of my control, and I allowed myself to relax in his grip.

My new benefactor hoisted me up into the passenger seat in the cab of what I now know to be a semi-trailer truck, but at the time, it could have been a carnivorous dinosaur for all the fear it instilled in me. In my reluctance to cooperate, I squealed in fear and flailed about, nipping him with my baby teeth. This only served to further irritate him, and he yelled at me and handled me roughly in response. The sheer height of my new perch terrified me. Having just spent most of my life under a porch, I had a fear of heights at that moment, which left me feeling terribly insecure.

I became dizzy and was on the verge of vomiting. I had a brief mental image of my birth mom teetering on the rusty bed frame in the back of her people's truck. The passenger's seat where the man placed me was covered with debris, greasy clothing, papers, and an open metal tool box. I wasn't able to settle properly to keep my balance. I saw a much safer area on the floor below the glove box, and I slithered down to nestle in among some discarded coffee cups and fast food wrappers where I proceeded to shake uncontrollably.

I recall trying to sleep, but my newly acquired travel anxiety prevented me from doing so, and I continued to shudder beyond my control. Eventually, out of sheer exhaustion, I actually did manage to zone out lightly and dreamed of Doug. Again, I don't remember my exact thoughts at the time, but there are a lot of very clear memories mixed with some confusion and fog related to that transitional time of my life. I'm sure it's because I'd yet to understand the human language and was barely out of infancy too. I probably expected Doug to reappear at any time and take me away from this strange man in whose great white dragon I was being held against my will. As I've pondered this, later in my life I realized that had it not been for this stranger, who knows what the cruel hand of fate would have dealt—a fate that I don't care to even guess about. Feeling like a prisoner for the first time since my confinement at my birth mom's house, I'd become the reluctant companion of a long distance hauler.

Dogs have a peculiar trait that is beyond our control. We tend to unconditionally love the humans who disappoint us. Regardless of what had transpired back in the town that led to my imprisonment within this new vehicle and with its warden, I loved Doug unconditionally, and a part of me always would. I was emotionally vulnerable back then, and for weeks after, I continued to expect him at any moment. Had we actually reunited, I can say for certain my forgiveness would have been instantaneous and without conditions. At that particular moment, beneath the dashboard of the truck, I was focused on the few good memories I had stored away of my three-week respite at Doug's place. I had already forgotten the debacle that had been our miserable car trip. Somehow I once again drifted off to sleep.

I was suddenly awakened as my new companion hollered loudly at someone using a strange talking device to do so. Because of my experience at the old house, I was accustomed to loud talking, so it didn't startle or frighten me. The talking device appeared to be a way for the driver to communicate with another person whom I didn't see. At first this struck me as odd, but I quickly got used to it. I didn't understand the nature of the animated conversations that took place at the time, yet I was able to ascertain that my new traveling companion used the moniker M. T. Nester or just plain Nester for short. I was given the impression that he was well liked as he appeared to be sending and receiving many friendly messages. Nester's momentary good humor and preoccupation with something other than myself allowed me to relax, and I happily returned to the *Doug* dream I was having before being woken up.

The air quality within the cab of the semi was moderately comfortable compared to Doug's car. I would have preferred the scent of grass instead of the oily smell coming down my way from the tool box and greasy rags on the seat just above me, but at least it wasn't hot. The ride was much smoother, and I was no longer being jolted about as I had been in Doug's old wreck with its lousy suspension. The more controlled climate allowed my stomach to settle too. By the time I awoke from my second or third nap, the nausea that had plagued me earlier was completely gone, and my appetite had returned. I perked up when I heard the sound of crackling cellophane as Nester struggled to open a package of cookies using his one free hand and his teeth as he drove. Immediately upon opening, I was able to identify the smell of shortbread sandwich cookies with peanut butter centers, which happened to be my favorites. Thinking about it now, it was probably too much of a coincidence for Nestor to have those cookies on hand, so I guess they were probably given to him by Doug as a going away goody for me—like some kind of a lame offering to ease his guilt for giving me away. Nester attempted to lure me up onto the seat beside him with one of the cookies, but I declined the offer, suspecting that it was a trick on his part. Finally giving up, he tossed the cookie down to me. It sat, uneaten, just inches from my nose. Fearful and confused at this sudden change of tactic, I was unwilling to accept his gift, deciding that to do so was not worth the risk. Furthering his growing annoyance at me for not taking the bait, I ignored him and instead concentrated on planning a means of escape should the opportunity present itself. As hard as I desperately tried, I was unable to keep my mind off the cookie, which had been inching its way closer to my snout from the vibration of the vehicle. Its sweet peanut smell enticed me unbearably, and it caused my saliva to escape in a long drool that streamed onto the floor mat, forming a small sticky puddle. Lest I be tempted to accept his offer, I averted my eyes and allowed my mind to drift off to happier times back at Doug's house.

Permitting my subconscious to take me to a state of peace or indifference was a technique I'd developed back at the old house as a way, I suppose, of controlling pain—both physical and emotional. You might say it was the equivalent of human self-hypnosis or a coping mechanism. Within the mental walls of this self-willed safety zone, I floated in a dreamlike existence and found solace in the soothing moments that had meant a lot to me during my short time with Doug. I recalled our last evening as we shared the two cans of corned beef hash and stared at the wall where the TV had once been, silently content with just being together. I thought about the rhythmic sound of his snoring that comforted me through the night, my toys that were regrettably left behind, and last but not least, the delicious smell of the early spring grass and how it felt on my paws as I ran back and forth.

I also remembered how proud I felt with Doug cheering me on. His enthusiastic coaching would prompt me to run even faster. I think at the time I would have done anything just to impress him and hear him praise me for it…

I was jolted from my self-imposed trance by the squeal of the semi's brakes as it pulled into a truck stop. My new person, Nester, grabbed the clipboard on the passenger seat and climbed down, leaving the door slightly ajar. I had already forgotten my earlier plan to escape. I was eager to stretch my legs, which were beginning to cramp from lack of exercise. Since I had to relieve myself anyway, I stepped over the cookie, and I followed him out of the cab. I nearly landed on my head when I jumped from the floorboard to the pavement below. After finding a suitable place to leave my *calling card*, I became distracted by all the interesting things the place had to offer. Feeling liberated, I let my curiosity lead the way. The place was teeming with rigs like the one I was traveling in. I'd never seen such a spectacle, being the inexperienced country bumpkin that I was. I was astounded at how tiny the humans seemed in comparison to the trucks. At a mere fraction of a human's size, I was able to explore freely as it appeared no one took notice of me. I darted under the rigs, and I managed, miraculously, to avoid harming myself as I dodged enormous tires that wheeled around in unpredictable patterns. As I explored, I kept trying to keep Nester in my peripheral vision. I was soon feeling more refreshed, so my thoughts turned to food; and I remembered the peanut butter cookie I'd refused, which was still sitting on the floor of his semi. I began following the trail I'd marked back to Nester's truck, but when I found it, although it's door was still ajar, I was unable to climb back up into the semi—an impossible feat for my small size back then. Suddenly, my nose picked up a new smell of meat carried along by the breeze. Following the scent, I headed toward what turned out to be a concession area, and my only hope of getting something to eat.

So far on the trip, being fed and watered had been somewhat of an iffy proposition for me. I wasn't sure what to do. I had no experience in providing for my own nourishment, particularly in an area of paved roads and parking lots. Instinct told me that if I just stood by the door, I would eventually be fed. My patience that day at the truck stop was ultimately rewarded. A warm grilled frankfurter was tossed out onto the pavement in front of me with my name on it. Then a bowl of water was lowered to my feet. I looked up, and there stood Nester, my new hero, smiling down at me. I regretted my earlier rejection of his cookie offering. With the hotdog safely tucked away in my gut, my bad attitude changed to one of gratitude, and I began seeing him in a new light as Nester's softer side was winning me over.

I could feel myself beginning to bond with Nester that day, but as it turned out, like Doug, he too abandoned me. Right after he fed and watered me, he tied me with a bungee cord to the leg of a picnic table just outside of the concession area. In disbelief, I watched as my new person turned and walked away; and after climbing into his rig, he hit the road and never looked back. My first thought was that he was a cad and a bounder, and I was so glad that I didn't take the cookie after all. Suddenly dejected and lost, my stomach began to hurt, and I was wishing I'd refused the hotdog too. One day, after I understood their language, I learned the whole story of what happened that day and why I didn't leave with Nester.

Nester had, in fact, really been kinder than I thought at the time. When he'd overheard Doug trying to sell me to the highest bidder back at the diner that morning, he'd taken pity on him—and me—and that's the reason he gave Doug enough money to buy a bus ticket. He then released Doug of the burden I presented by telling him he'd been looking for a dog just like me to ride shotgun on his long trucking hauls. Whether or not Nester actually intended to make me his traveling buddy remains unknown. The truth of the matter was that I obviously didn't travel well and never would be "the best traveling companion a truck driver could ever have" as Doug had proclaimed me to be when he'd put me up for bid back at the restaurant. After explaining the situation to the owner of the truck stop and one of the employees, he was promised that I'd be taken care of. The last time I saw Nester, he was sitting up in the lofty seat of his rig as it pulled out onto the busy highway with Country and Western music blasting away at full volume out the open driver's window. Unlike Doug, he didn't look back and wave.

A Port in the Storm

It is a mistake to look too far ahead. Only one link of the chain of destiny can be handled at a time.

—Winston Churchill

To my relief, my care was soon handed over to a truck stop mechanic who loved dogs and owned one of his own. His name was Ken, and under his watchful eye, I spent the remainder of that afternoon. As fate would have it, Ken was the son of my future *forever* Dad, so in hindsight, it was ironic that this was to become more than a casual encounter. I spent the rest of the workday tied by a leash to his workbench while he performed various truck repairs. He seemed very capable at what he did. He also talked to me a lot that afternoon as he worked under the hood of a giant metal beast. Now that I'm older, I realize he was trying to cheer me up, but I wasn't really paying all that much attention at the time. I was still clinging to the possibility that Doug would come walking in the door at any moment to take me back to his house up north. Confusion about where I was and why I was there left me unsure about making friends too easily. Ken appeared content to let me sulk and treated me as though he didn't notice it. Waiting and longing for Doug became too much of an effort for me, and I dozed off and on all afternoon. Each time I woke up, it was to fresh heartbreak. Once fully conscious, I'd remember Doug and his abandonment hours earlier.

When I wasn't sleeping, I carefully examined every detail of my surroundings. I could tell from the scent of Ken's work station, clothing, and personal items that I wasn't the only dog he'd been dealing with, and that another dog sometimes occupied the area beneath the workbench where I now lay. Ken seemed to know when I needed to be taken outdoors to do my *business*, and he made sure that I had plenty of cold water available for drinking. It sure beat drinking lukewarm water from a plastic tub on the floor mat of Doug's car.

I didn't understand at the time, but since the story has been told repeatedly over the years, this is what actually happened that day: At the end of his work day, Ken spoke to his employer on my behalf, generously offering to assume the responsibility of my welfare for the weekend. His intention at the time was to take me to a haven called the shelter on the following Monday. The shelter was closed for the weekend, and since it was after five o'clock on a Friday afternoon, Ken's offer was gladly accepted by his boss. When Ken put me into his truck, I had no will left to fight, so I didn't resist. The truck was completely covered in dog scent, so intense that it made me very nervous. My instincts warned me of a possible territorial infringement. Thankfully, because I was exhausted anyway, I immediately fell asleep and remember nothing of that ride home with Ken.

It'd been a long day, in spite of all the napping I'd done. At the time, it seemed like a lifetime had gone by since that morning when Doug and I first set out for the place he called Florida. Since being adopted and then abandoned by both Doug and Nester the trucker, all the activity of the afternoon and Ken's kindness had been a welcome diversion for me. My memories of Doug were dimming but far from over. I'm grateful that all this heartache occurred during the early developmental stage of my life. I believe that my youthful resilience helped me through that difficult time, and the experience has strengthened me.

I woke up when the pickup jolted to a stop at Ken's home. As I crossed the threshold of Ken's house, I caught the clearly identifiable scent that meant the presence of a not-so-friendly dog and understood I was about to be encroaching on his domain. At the old house, stray or feral dogs sometimes invaded our territory and temporarily wreaked havoc until my birth mom was able to challenge and drive them off. More often than not, when they realized we had no food to steal, they left of their own accord. However, with Ken by my side and with his apparent permission, I determined that it was safe to enter the home. I was soon fed the best food I'd had in my entire life, apart from the nourishment my birth mom had provided me with while it lasted. I was to later learn that it was canned food that was expressly made for dogs! Doug would have been astonished at the idea!

The other dog that resided at Ken's house was being fed in a separate room that afternoon because it was anticipated that he might take me for an uninvited intruder. Ken thought it would be best to explain my presence to him in private before formal introductions were made. I could see the dog through the door when it was cracked open. He was a large white dog with a pink nose—an immensely imposing creature from my much lower vantage point. Ken called him Champ. When he was released from his temporary bedroom prison, Champ made a grand display of power by lunging at me. Ken desperately yanked back on the leash in an effort to maintain control of the situation. Not intimidated, I boldly approached the restrained tyrant and came nose to nose with him then flipped over onto my back in deference to his seniority. Perhaps it was the fact that I was merely a puppy that posed no threat that kept Champ from biting my tiny head off at the very moment of our introduction. Fortunately, my instinctive posturing in subservience, a universal signal of canine submission, diffused a potentially dangerous situation.

As I think about it now, I must have been quite a sight and smell that day as I had yet to be properly cleaned up from my unfortunate incident in Doug's car earlier that morning. I was too young to have cared about my appearance, yet even I could still smell the residual odor of my earlier meatloaf sickness. Although Champ rebuffed my repeated attempts to get to know him better, he seemed to sense that the situation was out of my control and did exhibit a lot of tolerance of my presence throughout the rest of the evening.

Shortly after that, I met Ken's wife, Brooke, and their two kids, Sara and Richie, who were all returning home for the day. Meeting these children was my first encounter with little humans, and I thought they were utterly fascinating. Richie, an eight year old and the larger of the two, startled me with his sudden boyish movements, which from his perspective were intended to be innocent rough play. Since I was too young to understand his youthful aggression, I balked at returning his challenge. Instead, I guess because she was a female like me, I was more drawn to the gentle attention of his six-year-old sister Sara who appeared to be more sensitive to my shyness and exhaustion. The similarity of their small stature to mine gave me a sense of belonging—a sensation I had missed since the loss of my siblings.

I was given a bath that night at the insistence of Brooke. This would be my first bath ever. I really enjoyed being immersed into warm water, but the suds tasted bitter. Although Ken was careful not to get them in my eyes, some of those suds did seep in and they stung. Afterward, I was wrapped in a soft towel that smelled wonderful. Champ was an attentive observer throughout the procedure. I even noticed that he cracked a dog smile, which is a particular facial expression unlike that of a human smile that only dogs can identify. At the time, I took this as a good sign that maybe he did have a friendlier side. I can't imagine why, as there was no resemblance, but something about Champ reminded me of my birth mom. Maybe it was his imposing size. Champ never did warm up to me fully during my weekend there. He didn't appreciate it cither when I tried to cozy up to him for some *maternal* warmth—something I naively thought he could provide me with. And it didn't go unnoticed by me that his lip curled up into another smug dog smile when Ken showed him a lot of special attention and kept his distance from me, so Champ wouldn't get jealous.

Back then I resented Champ's hostility toward me. Now that I have a family of my own though, I can appreciate the resentment I must have stirred up inside him. In all honesty, Champ was a pretty good sport under the circumstances. In hindsight, I now believe that at that time, Ken was probably also a little reluctant to get too attached to me. Still, I felt very needy for human contact that first night, so I gravitated toward Ken's little daughter Sara for some human companionship. She insisted on dubbing me "Princess." Because my understanding of their language was so limited then, their plans for my future meant nothing to me; and I took my captivity in stride, having no other choice anyway. It really wasn't so unpleasant being held prisoner by this delightful child companion. I don't remember my exact perception of my captivity within Ken's home at that moment in time. I think I probably believed that Doug would be coming to fetch me at any moment from a play date. Meanwhile, Sara's Dad made it clear to her from the beginning that my future destination was the shelter, and my stay there was temporary. I didn't know the implications of that statement, but it seemed to have quite an impact on young Sara. Her whole demeanor would change to sadness whenever he reminded her of this. I've since come to understand what the shelter is, and the unfortunate consequence of being a resident dog there when no one steps forward to adopt you. I know this because the family has talked about it from time to time over the years—how close I came to being a shelter dog.

Later that evening, I was yearning for Doug again. I found solace underneath Sara's bed. Since she was the one who'd been willing to step forward and be my interim protector, it was decided that I would spend the night in Sara's bedroom. Eventually, I slept but only after crying for Doug until the early morning hours. One of the things that helped to comfort me was that my night spent under Sara's bed was incredibly comfortable. My bed of lush pile carpeting kept me dry and warm, and I was finally lulled to sleep by the sound of Sara's steady breathing. As the dawn broke in the morning sky, I crawled out from below and feeling the need for human bonding—something Doug started—I crawled into bed, wedging myself between Sara and her fake toy animals. She slept through my invasion of her space, oblivious to my presence. As I rhythmically inhaled the sweet baby-like breath that came from her child's nose and mouth inches from mine, I managed to drift back off to puppy dreamland.

Regardless of my many disappointments and let downs, I still had hope for a brighter future in my puppy heart, and yet all I could do was wait and see what was in store for me. At that time, I had an instinct that my stay at that home would not be my final destination. Until then, my life experiences had left an impact beyond that of what most other dogs have to bear in their entire lifetimes. As I see it now, if anything good could be said about the havoc of my early life, it would be that it encouraged me to be more observant of the world around me and see things beyond my own selfish needs and desires. As it turned out, my stay in that house was going to connect me to something more permanent. Although they wouldn't be my *forever* people, they became part of my extended family, and I would always remain a part of their lives.

I couldn't believe my luck that first morning at Ken's, when I was fed for the second time since arriving the previous night. Back then, being fed in the morning was highly unusual for me. At Doug's house, mealtime was an evening-only event, so I'd be half starved by the time I did get fed. Even that had been an improvement over near starvation due to my dependence on a birth mom who had been losing the ability to provide nourishment to an overgrown puppy during my life back at the old house. I don't know if that had anything to do with the fact that food became an obsession and preoccupation for me for the rest of my life.

On that first full day at Ken's, it rained cats and dogs (I've always been tickled when I've heard Mom or Dad use that expression). Other than a quick walk around the neighborhood, Champ and I were stuck inside. Ken's house was big compared to Doug's, so I had a lot of exploring to do under the watchful scrutiny of Champ who eyed me suspiciously from his sentry post by the kitchen door. The humans were in a whirlwind of activity with a definite purpose in mind. I had no way of knowing for sure, but it appeared to be preparation of some sort, and I feared that it might have something to do with me. Trying to figure out what it meant, I looked to Champ for a clue, as I had often done with my birth mom. If he knew what was going on, his poker-face gave me no clues and he avoided any voluntary interaction with me. Unable to relax and panting incessantly, I was sent to Sara's room along with Sara, who was getting in the way of the adults anyway. We occupied the time by spending a delightful afternoon playing with her toys on her bedroom floor and having a tea party with her stuffed animals—ridiculous imposters that didn't fool me for an instant, but apparently, she believed them to be real. Playing with Sara helped to distract and amuse me, and the day flew by quickly. The evening followed the same schedule as the one before with the exception that I wasn't given a bath.

The First Day of the Rest of My Life

Coming together is a beginning; keeping together is progress; working together is success.

—Henry Ford

The first day of the rest of my life began on Easter Sunday, April 19, 1992. I know this from hearing Mom mention it so often over the years. Things were about to get considerably better for me, although none of the players knew it yet. It all began on my second morning at Ken's. I was lying pressed up against Sara, enjoying the rhythm of her steady breathing. As I laid there, I could see out of the window across the room, and something about the smell of the air or the appearance of the outdoors took me momentarily back to being curled up with my birth mom in our box bed. The thought was fleeting though, as that time period of my infancy was fast becoming a distant and foggy memory, only to regain clarity in these last days of my life. Even thoughts of Doug were becoming fewer, but since I'd only been separated from him for less than two days, those thoughts would take more time to become distant memories.

After Champ and I were taken by Ken for an early walk, I returned to my place in Sara's bed beside her and slept some more until the rest of the family got up. My thoughts of Doug began again, and I hoped that soon he would come to pick me up, so we could go back home. I reasoned that I would miss Sara, of course, but being with Doug again would help me get over her. As I zoned out deep into my puppy daydreams, I thought about running in some grass. I remember feeling a deep longing that morning for the days I'd spent with Doug in the yard of his house. Since the sun was out and the rain gone, I hoped I would be allowed some time in Ken's yard, which I had admired earlier that morning on our walk.

Once the entire family got up, no one was idle for any length of time. I was disappointed when Sara wasn't available to play since the whole family was focused on getting ready to go to a place called church. I hoped that whatever church meant, it wouldn't require my participation as I sensed it involved motor vehicle travel. Maybe it was the transfer of car keys from one hand to another or something someone said that triggered an association to car travel, but I was afraid that I might be included in the plans. (Throughout my life, my parents have continued this tradition of going to a place called church; but to my relief, I've never had to go with them when they do.)

I've come to realize, dogs have a strong intuition and; over time, some of us have even mastered the ability to understand human language. Additionally, we're often able to solve complex problems and have used that ability for good—though usually not getting the credit. But sometimes our effort is acknowledged and has even earned us the title of "hero" when our instincts have led us to take preventive or preemptive measures, depending on the circumstances. I believe, at almost four months of age, my attention to nuances, though subtle at times, were just the beginning of the development of the ability to discern what was about to happen at any given moment. It began as single word clues, then word association with certain human behavior patterns. Although my early attempts to comprehend human dialog were primitive at best, eventually I came to understand it fluently. Through the years, I honed that natural gift, and it served me well throughout my life, for good and bad. Although I didn't understand back then and was confused about my environment during those days of my early youth, I've since been able to piece together a good understanding of what transpired.

Eventually, Champ was brought indoors after being given first dibs on a substantial amount of outdoor play time. I'd watched most of it from the living room window and longed to go join him. I now understand that there was only one dog run and leash available, so we had to take turns. When they made the dog transfer at last, I was elated to be outdoors and sucked in as much of the fresh smell of nature as my lungs could take in. The yard was completely covered with beautiful grass. The aroma was spectacular—even better than that of Doug's place. The trees in Ken's yard were fully leafed out, and the lawn was almost completely surrounded by woods. There were no snow drifts or piles anywhere, all having dissolved in the warmth of the spring thaw and the rain of the previous day. When I'd been taken on a neighborhood walk earlier, I'd briefly noticed a few subtle changes to the house and lawn that hadn't been there the day before. Now outside on my own, I had the luxury of taking in these new sights without being pulled briskly along on the end of a leash. An arrangement of floral bouquets, which now graced the steps of the porch, caught my eye, as it was the first time I ever saw flowers. Even as a puppy, I was able to recognize beauty, and I saw and smelled it that day everywhere I looked. While I was tied in the yard, I sprinted back and forth on my short legs until I grew tired and flopped down, spread eagle. As my chin rested flat on the ground, I picked up the scent of what turned out to be a plastic candy-filled egg. The egg had apparently been deliberately hidden and was intended for an egg hunt that had been planned by the humans for later that day. Over the years I've since grown used to this strange human custom that apparently delights children who participate in it. Even though I wasn't hungry at that moment, I found and ate the contents of two more jelly bean–filled eggs before I threw up behind the wood pile. Feeling guilty, I looked up at the window and saw Champ, eyeing me with a look of disdain from the inside. I figured I'd be in trouble, but nothing was mentioned when I was brought indoors.

As the family got ready to leave for that place called church, it was decided at a family conference that Ken would remain behind. The reason for that decision I'm sure was that I could not be trusted alone and unsupervised since I was unacquainted with the house rules. Also, I would need protection from Champ. Apparently, I was still subject to the potential threat of having my head bitten off by him, and he was still too unpredictable where I was concerned. Ken had made a special breakfast for the family while I'd been outside on the dog run. After I was allowed back inside, I could smell the residual odor of bacon that hung in the air, and I began to salivate even though I wasn't hungry. Ken basted a couple of small dog biscuits in leftover bacon grease for me and Champ and warned us not to tell Brooke. I didn't understand him, but I readily agreed as I eagerly devoured the biscuit. Later, the smell of a ham baking in the oven drove me crazy, and I found it hard to think of anything else. I looked forward to eating the ham, although I wasn't going to be getting any of it. I just didn't know that at the time.

By early afternoon, I observed that Ken's family kept looking out the window in expectation. I was caught up in the anticipation and watched too, out of curiosity. Champ seemed to also be full of excitement, although he had the advantage of previous experience, so his perspective was different than mine. He remained aloof where I was concerned, so I gave up trying to look to him for guidance. Eventually, I became more bored than curious when nothing of interest happened, so I crawled under Sara's bed to take a nap. There, I thought about Doug and how happy I would be to see him when he came to get me.

My *forever* Mom and Dad were the first guests to arrive that day. The commotion startled me awake. I peeked out at the disturbance from the vantage point of my under-the-bed sanctuary, which gave me a superb view of the kitchen through Sara's open bedroom door. When my future Mom and Dad came through the entry, Champ barked like crazy, and the family rushed to greet them with loud voices and laughter. Sara excitedly told them about me and immediately betrayed my secret location to them. Then I heard Ken's voice saying something about the shelter, a place where I was going to be taken the next day. As I listened to them talking by the kitchen doorway, I knew the conversation was all about me. I began to tremble in panic as I sensed another change was about to take place for which I had no control. I remember thinking that I hoped Doug would be coming to get me soon!

No longer cleverly hidden, I wasn't surprised when Mom entered the room and right away knelt to look under the bed at me. At first, I shook with fear and was reluctant to come out; but the gentle nurturing tone of her voice wore me down, and she managed to coax me into her outstretched arms. (After meeting Sara and Brooke, I was beginning to realize that human females could be trusted after all, and that those women back at the old house had been the exceptions.) I know it wasn't the same for her, but for me it was love at first hug when Mom held me. I knew I had to have her for my *forever* Mom at that very moment. I felt the same about Dad when I saw him. He's a big man but not in a scary way. He's quiet and strong. I sensed at our first meeting that he was a human with a lot of integrity. He had a way about him at that moment that made me feel safe and secure. As he looked me over, I felt the beginning spark of bonding. I had no problem when he took his turn at holding me. Maybe my memory of that first meeting is slightly embellished for the better, but I offer no apologies for that. I've allowed myself the luxury of remembering it this way as my devotion for my family has grown.

I don't know the precise moment that I began feeling it, but my instinct told me that Mom and Dad were, in some way, going to become a permanent part of my life, yet I wasn't sure how. Maybe it was just some of that budding dog sense I was thinking of earlier. I get goose bumps when I think about it now—that my future was sealed that day, and I was about to get the best gift a dog could ever have. I was going to go home with those two humans to stay forever! At that time, I was too young to appreciate how close I had come to being a shelter dog! Young Sara's hold on me was collapsing like a house of cards, and she took the news badly when it was made clear to her that I was going home with her grandparents, and she'd be sleeping alone without me that night. I tried to comfort her, but I didn't exactly have a full grip of the facts myself. Since that time, I've become convinced that if I'd been given enough time with Ken's family, they would have eventually loved me enough to let me stay with them rather than taking me to the shelter.

During many conversations at extended family dinners over the years, I've overheard Ken say he wouldn't have gone through with taking me to the shelter as he'd originally planned. In fact, by that Easter Sunday morning in 1992, he and Brooke had already decided to keep me—they were just going to wait until after the big family dinner to break the good news to Richie and Sara. However, when Ken saw how quickly Mom and Dad bonded to me when they arrived, letting me go home with them seemed to make a lot more sense at the time, and Brooke agreed. Sara was never to learn about this until many years later.

The next most wonderful thing that happened to me that day was that Mom named me Jessie! Everybody began calling me that immediately, which seemed weird at first, but I liked the way it sounded. Mom has often reminded me over the course of my life that it was the same name given to her birth family's dog—a dog that had been loved and adored by all who knew her but was now deceased. (I've always tried to live up to that honor. From everything Mom has told me about her family's dog, I would like to have known her.) Unfortunately for Sara, this meant that I would no longer be known as Princess, of course, which had been just a temporary name and even then, only she used it anyway. It had never really caught on with the rest of her family lest it mislead Sara about the temporary nature of my stay there. Initially, she balked at my name change but later that day finally conceded that my new real name was Jessie. Sara and I had a secret of our own though, because for years after that she continued to call me Princess whenever she visited, and I got to sleep with her in the guestroom. As my first real playmate, she had that right. As she got older though, to my regret, she eventually stopped calling me Princess.

Later that Easter Sunday in 1992, more relatives arrived with their children. They were cousins, aunts, and uncles who belonged to the family, and they were allowed to pet me and pick me up although my new *forever* Mom and Dad cautioned them to be gentle. I loved the sound of the children's tiny voices when they exclaimed "Jessie!" over and over again and crowded around me as their sweet breath filled my nostrils. They jostled for position and fell over each other to get close enough to play with me. I squirmed and laughed in delight as they tickled me with their gentle tiny hands. I particularly remember that moment because it almost brought me back in time to when my siblings and I playfully wrestled in our puppy pileups under the porch back at the old house. Those were the few times at that place that life had seemed almost bearable.

Among the steady flow of relatives that arrived that day, there were those who brought along the family dogs that belonged to them. After controlled introductions were made, the newly arrived dogs examined me under the protection of my new parents. Eventually, we dogs were let loose into the back yard to get to know each other better. We had an awesome time chasing and sniffing each other. Having been warned, they were mindful of my diminutive size and treated me with caution. Mostly ignoring me, and instead turning to one another in familiarity, they roughly nipped one another's ears and legs and chased each other mercilessly. At first, I was alarmed at the loud yelps and barking, but then I realized it was just part of their roughhousing. No dog was actually getting hurt. While out there, we dogs also hunted for candy-filled eggs that we hoped might still be hidden in the yard after the egg hunt that had taken place earlier. We'd watched the event with curiosity from the window inside. I myself knew what the contents of those eggs tasted like, and I suspect the other dogs did too. The older dogs did manage to find a couple of well hidden yet undiscovered eggs. Since I had mine earlier that morning, I didn't mind not sharing—which was good because they didn't offer me any.

I loved watching the bigger dogs play King of the Mountain, with the wood pile being the mountain or the yard tractor being the mountain. When they got tired of that, they began to play-fight over some of Champ's yard toys. Although I didn't really participate in the games due to my size, I stood on the sidelines and barked encouragingly, rooting for the underdog but happy with any outcome. All this helped to keep us dogs preoccupied and blissfully unaware of the ham dinner that was being enjoyed by the humans inside the house—the very meal I'd anticipated with great relish but would not be partaking in. When the dogs were finally rounded up and brought back into the house, the table had already been cleared and the leftovers were packed away and out of sight. In spite of what the humans chose to believe, we dogs weren't one bit fooled about the food we'd missed out on and there was resentment all around amongst us. All was soon forgotten and forgiven though because Ken made sure we all got an ample dish of canned dog food and some vanilla ice cream for each of us for desert!

That evening, when it was time to leave with my new Mom and Dad, I reluctantly got into the car, not wanting the fun I'd had that day to end. Also, I dreaded another road trip. After starting out seated on Mom's lap, I soon slithered off of her and made my way down onto her feet. Then wedging myself into the furthest corner of the floorboards possible, I proceeded to shudder, pant, and drool my way to a catatonic trance, tuning out any words of comfort and continued what would become a lifelong traveling habit of mine. To my relief, the ride was a short one as not long after, we arrived at my new home, and I quickly regained my composure once my feet were planted safely on the ground. As I entered Mom and Dad's house, I set about exploring every room and made it a point to touch every piece of furniture inside with my wet nose as an initiation rite of my own. By doing this, I was sealing my covenant with Mom and Dad and establishing my right of tenancy in what would now be my *forever* home!

There's No Place Like Home

The dog represents all that is best in man.

—Etienne Charlet

During my entire fifteen years of life, my family hasn't wavered much in their annual cycles and routines. The consistency of our lives has been a great comfort. Although they've occasionally left someone in charge of me for brief periods of time, I have no doubt they will return for me. Mom has a peculiar habit of saying "See you later!" whenever she leaves the house. She always comes back eventually, so her saying it is like she's reminding me of our special bond that will never break. I think she says this as much for her own reassurance as mine. It's given me a strong sense of security for which I'm profoundly grateful, as I don't think I could have easily lived the vagabond life of a homeless dog or a foster dog. Perhaps because of my humble beginnings, I could have mustered up the will to survive on my own, and I did have some skills to help me do so. But the truth is that from the beginning, I had a big need to love and be loved back. I personally required the stability and security of a *forever* family in order to thrive. I don't know this for certain, but I'd be willing to bet that most, if not all dogs, feel the same way I do about this. Sadly, because we have no voice that can be understood by the human race, there is no way of making our wishes known.

As soon as possible after my adoption at four months of age, I was taken to see Dr. King, our local vet, for my first ever examination. The minute I was escorted into the reception area of his clinic, I was bombarded with so many animal smells that I feared the worst. The floor was covered in multiple dog scents, and I kept trying to get up on one of the chairs, but my folks wouldn't allow it. So I sat on the floor in the lobby in front of Mom and Dad and shook till my teeth chattered. I could hear the constant barking coming from behind the closed doors, and I knew it meant trouble. A lady came in with a cat in a carrier and sat in the waiting area near us. I kept straining on my leash to go check it out, just out of curiosity, but Dad hung on to my collar and wouldn't let me budge. The lady gave me dirty looks and held on to the carrier as the cat meowed within.

Eventually, we were led further into the building through a door, and I was lifted by Dad onto a stainless steel examining table, which although it appeared to be clean, smelled strongly of another dog. It was slippery, and I had difficulty getting my footing, so Dad made me lie down. The strong odor of antiseptic that stung my nostrils was freaking me out, and I kept trying to get off the table, but Mom and Dad held me firmly there till a man in a white coat walked in. I don't know what exactly it was about him, but I accepted his authority over me without question; and obediently, I laid on my side as he poked every square inch of me and shone a bright light into my eyes, my mouth, and pulled my tongue out to give it a good going over. My ears were next. He said I had ear mites and put some medication on a swab, jabbing it deep into my ears. Some of the poking hurt, and I felt some sharp pricks on my leg when he stuck a needle in it a couple of times. I thought that was kind of mean, but throughout my life,

I've had to go through this at least once a year. I've determined it's something that is required of me, and the best course of action is not to fight it. Actually, I have noticed that over the years, Dr. King is kind and affectionate toward me, as is the lady who greets us each time we first arrive. I can always tell, by how animated and excited she reacts when I walk in, that I am a very special guest and they are happy to see me.

On my very first visit back when I was a puppy, we learned of my probable Christmas or New Year's birth date, and that I was a Collie-Beagle mix. At that time, Dr. King estimated that my future adult weight would probably be around seventy pounds. Apparently, he was able to determine that from the size of my paws. To his credit, his prediction came pretty close to the actual sixty-five pounds that I've maintained all my adult life. On my first veterinary visit, Dr. King discovered that I had an infestation of ticks. They were removed, but as we tended to have deer ticks in the woods in Massachusetts, this was a problem that required medication throughout my life, and it didn't always work. At that first veterinary visit, I was given a clean bill of health and some shots, which stung me, but I soon forgot the pain when the lady at the front desk gave me a treat. After a trip to the town hall, Dad presented me with a beautiful new red nylon collar on which he attached the tags they'd given him. When we got home that day, Dad took a picture of me and Mom sitting on the stone wall in fond embrace. I've always loved looking at that picture over the years where it sits on the fireplace mantel. It was taken before Mom's hair changed color from brown to yellow.

I returned to Dr. King's office for another visit a couple of months later, at which time I was rendered incapable of bearing any offspring. I don't have any recollection about the treatment I received at that visit, but I do recall waking up from the best sleep I ever had. I was covered with a warm blanket, and I wondered where I was for a few moments till I fully woke up and remembered Dad bringing me there. Dad picked me up and brought me home shortly afterward with a small incision held together by stitches that healed soon after. The strange cone I was forced to wear around my neck during that time was a nuisance, but a necessity, I was told and I eventually gave up trying to slither out of it. Years later, I know my folks pined away at the thought of having more of me and sometimes regretted having had me "fixed," as they called it. The term always confused me because I hadn't realized before my surgery that I was broken. Even if I had been allowed to reproduce, there would have been no guarantee of my giving birth to another dog as wonderful as me, so it was a wise decision at the time.

As I lie here now, an entire fifteen years of a long dog's lifetime behind me, I'm glad that I'll be able to end it all, surrounded by my favorite things and my favorite people by my side. I only wish I'd been able to hang in there until spring, but my end is very near, and I wouldn't have been physically able to enjoy the family Easter celebration anyway or climb the steps when we got there. I'll miss all of them. I've enjoyed watching Ritchie and Sara grow up over the years, and whenever I see them, we reconnect as if we were never apart. Another thing that comforts me is that Dad promised me once (and I've often overheard Dad promise this to Mom too) that when the time came for me to "be put down," he would not put me into a car, the one thing I hated the most, and take me to the clinic. I even heard him say that he would be willing to pay whatever it took to have the deed done in my own home where I felt the safest. I'm not judging other people's choices here, but my Dad understood my traveling phobia enough to appreciate the unnecessary discomfort that one final car ride would add to my physical pain.

I overheard Mom tell Dad that she called the clinic this morning, and that Dr. King is away on vacation. The doctor's assistant told Mom that my symptoms are normal for a dying dog, and that the doctor noted in my file that he didn't expect me to live much longer, and that was over six months ago. Mom declined the assistant's offer to interrupt Dr. King at his vacation residence because he'd said the same thing to Mom when we were at my annual visit last spring. The doctor's assistant told her to call the clinic when she was ready to "put me down," and that the vet on call could do it. Mom started crying when she told Dad that. She seemed to think they weren't very sensitive, but Dad told Mom that it was just part of their job. I guess Dr. King won't be surprised when I don't show up for my physical this spring…

During my first few days with my *forever* Mom and Dad, I was slowly made aware of what they expected of me. Apparently, most of the house rules were in stark contrast to those I'd learned in the past three weeks at Doug's, which were few and far between, so I had some fresh learning to do. I was downgraded in the pecking order in some way that was unclear to me, rendering me slightly below humans. This confused me as while I was living with Doug, we'd been equal in status, or at least I perceived it to be so. The day I arrived to live here at my *forever* home, I began to learn my first word. "No!" was repeated over and over that first evening and again constantly for several days after. Because it was shouted immediately after so many different things that I did, it took quite a while to figure out its exact meaning. Over the next few weeks, though, my position in the family unit became clearer as were their expectations. Thankfully, I was a quick learner and eager to please. I messed up a lot, but my new parents were compassionate people too, and as was always the case, my misdeed was quickly forgiven. Sometimes, though, my mistake was serious enough that Mom gave me the silent treatment for a while first. Eventually, I learned to be obedient at all times— at least most of the time. Early on, my *forever* Mom and Dad were pleasantly surprised when they realized I came fully house-trained. The unexpected bonus was my insistence on being taken to the woods at the edge of the lawn to do my *business*, so I wouldn't soil the yard. They didn't know it at the time, but they had Doug to thank for that.

It was understandable too that until I learned to behave to at least a minimal degree of decorum and not wreak havoc like puppies tend to do, I would be watched closely. My boundaries and limitations were not so hard as to confuse or overburden me, and as it turned out, I eventually became a model family member. As a learning puppy, I actually enjoyed the structure of having rules and the rewards that came with obeying them. I looked forward to each day of instruction as I was presented with additional challenges. I was given new toys and quickly forgot the ones I'd left behind at Doug's. I even found that I could go for days without even thinking about Doug! Mom's and Dad's willingness not to sweat the small stuff and pick their battles with me made all our lives much easier. As their love for me grew, my missteps mattered less and less, and the time soon came when Mom considered me to be a perfect specimen in every way. I heard her tell that to Dad one day. I didn't know what it meant, but I guessed it was a good thing as they both beamed at me when she said it. It turned out that they both grew to love me more over the course of my lifetime than they ever dreamed they could love another species.

With all these memories swirling around in my head, I'm unable to put them into any chronological order. I don't remember all the details of every little event in my life. Once my existence became more stable and secure with my forever family, my life is a big, mostly happy, jumble of experiences. Like humans, a dog's life takes them through phases until full maturity is reached, at which time the exact timeline of events isn't as important as the experiences themselves. There are experiences that stand out—both good and bad. The ones that have resurfaced over and over in my mind during my life are the ones that have had the most impact in shaping my character and helping to sustain me. Those are the ones I tend to be focusing on and doing this gives me peace.

Part 2

As her tail thumped rhythmically against the floor, an ear twitched, and her legs moved slightly as though they were running. So it was when Jessie dreamed.

Life and Love from My Perspective

If you have men who will exclude any of God's creatures from the shelter of compassion and pity, you will have men who will deal likewise with their fellow men.

—Francis of Assisi

Although I was extremely content and satisfied with my *forever* family from the moment they took me in, I sensed at the time that the reverse didn't always hold true. I may have been only a puppy during our early months together, but I was able to sense the subtle nuances that at times left me feeling unsettled. It could have been the stressful tones of human conversation or an abrupt "No!" at something I'd done. Whatever I did to provoke it, I could tell when they weren't happy. It could have been the frown on a face that usually wore a smile at my approach or just my observation of their body language as they cleared away the latest carnage I'd wrought on what was once a prized family possession. I've heard them tell other people over the years that back then, they sometimes questioned the spontaneous decision to take me into their household. However, they're always quick to point out that in hindsight, the blessings of my participation in their lives have far outweighed the occasional pitfalls.

I've thought a lot about this in my old age, and I've concluded that dogs have a type of unconditional love that begins the instant she is chosen by her forever family. The dog's love starts off big and stays big, continuing to increase rapidly to the point where she would gladly die for her human. In order to receive this love from a dog, nothing is required from the dog's human family—it is absolutely unconditional. Of course this doesn't really seem fair, but it's the way a dog has been hardwired by God. However, if the dog's love *is* reciprocated, the human will probably merit extra affection, but mutual adoration isn't necessary. I think it's sad to know that some dogs have an unrequited love for the humans who posses and abuse them. Such was the case with my birth mom and her people, I believe.

In contrast, the kind of love the human species has to offer their newly acquired pet is initially not so unconditional and is a bit more restrained. Only time will tell if the animal will continue to perform to the satisfaction of the human. Human love for a dog starts with an attraction to the particular appearance of a dog when it is first considered for adoption. Some people wouldn't even seriously entertain the adoption of a dog outside of a desired breed. They have their reasons, and I'm not judging them since even purebreds can become orphans despite their supposed superiority. Other humans can see straight through to the heart and soul of a dog, and the outward appearance is merely superficial. And there are those humans who gladly adopt dogs who would otherwise be deemed misfits, whether it is due to homeliness, physical deficiency due to interbreeding, or the genetic result of unsterilized and unrestrained dogs of different breeds. To the latter group of potential dog adopters, even a dog's age is inconsequential, and those people are willing to dispense with the joys of cuddling with a cute puppy. Instead, they are more than willing to give an old dog a chance to relearn about life within the confines of a loving family unit.

Whichever method is used to obtain a dog, at the very early stage of ownership, human love sees the glass as half full. The expectations are always positive, and the people choose to see only the good and worthy attributes of their new arrival. I believe this was the case with Doug. This kind of love is often referred to as Puppy Love. Once the initial euphoria has worn off though, a dog's performance becomes an issue; and if tolerance and patience are employed at that stage and an occasional misstep can be overlooked, the human's true love starts to grow steadily. Usually the rate of this growth accelerates rapidly until the level of respect and bonding between family members and the dog reaches its zenith. Yes, eventually, as it is with a dog's love, human love will crest. The humans will, by then, be willing to fall on the sword for their dog, as well as they would for any other member of the family. At that stage of human love, the dog is well entrenched in the family unit, and the loss of this pet is one of serious emotional consequence.

Unfortunately, this good case scenario doesn't always play out in real life, and a dog that doesn't make the grade in the eyes of her human is mistreated, ignored, or the human gives up trying too soon and abandons the dog. This was how it had been with both Doug and Nester. As hard as it can be for a dog lover to understand how this can be, it remains true that some humans fail to consider the seriousness of the commitment needed to provide all that an animal will need. If only people gave more thought to this important decision, stopped acting on impulse, and didn't ignore the red flags, more dogs would be spared the emotional pain and physical discomforts they endure under the imprisonment of a delinquent owner. I've heard Mom and Dad discussing this from time to time, and it saddens me to think some of those dogs might be my long lost siblings of years ago. I believe, as my parents do, that the creator of all of us, or

God as Mom calls him, is disappointed when he sees humans treating animals cruelly. I heard Mom say that in the beginning, God charged humans to be stewards or caretakers of us, not abusers. Even an animal that's about to be slaughtered for food is supposed to be given a certain degree of consideration in the process so as to lessen any fear or discomfort it might experience just prior to its death. Clearly, this is because animals do have feelings, and fears and should be regarded as worthy of kindness by people who control the animal's fate. No doubt, a human who exhibits the capacity to be cruel to animals will most likely do the same to their fellow humans too—some who cannot even speak for themselves. I know in my heart that when all is said and done, God's justice will be served toward them. (That's what Mom says.)

These are issues I've pondered over the last few months, especially when I've been too achy and sick to do much of anything else; and it's helped me to make sense of all the things that I've seen, both good and bad, during my lifetime. Some are things I've overheard being said by my parents and other people, and I'm in full agreement with them. Now I understand what Mom meant when she said, "Dogs are people too," whenever others accused her of treating me with too much consideration.

A Fresh Start

Deal with your servant according to your love and teach
me your decrees.

—Psalm 119:124

When I first came to live with Mom and Dad, not much was
expected of me. In time, my expected duties, which were already
hardwired into my species and instinctive, would come naturally
to me. No formal security training was required. Eventually, I was
expected to guard and protect their premises by barking to alert
them if intruders approached or wake them up if the house was
on fire. These were things I actually already knew about because
of my birth mom having been a guard dog and the experience
I'd had during my brush with death-by-fire while tied to the old
house of my early youth. Both of these experiences proved to be
helpful in adding to the knowledge I needed to have in performing
my new duties. I was also required to be ready at a moment's
notice to shower my humans with unabashed devotion, to imbue
them with shameless amounts of love, and exhibit faithfulness in
all I did for them. They also expected my instant companionship
whenever they so desired whether or not I was in the mood. This
was a moot point however as I was always up for this anyway.
As their companion, I was expected to be highly amused and
responsive to their jokes and antics, and above all, always do as I
was told—at least most of the time.

In return for my devotion, they promised to be available to me
for my emotional needs. They too were required to laugh at all of
my jokes and antics and promise to love and care for me always. As
my compensation for performing my duties, I was allowed access
to the interior of the house, to sit on the floor—preferably at
Mom or Dad's feet—should they suddenly require my attention.
At first, my use of the furniture or the bed was forbidden (a rule
that would change), and I was to eat lesser food, for which I
was expected to show an inordinate level of appreciation even
though it was not the hot homecooked meal that Mom and Dad
were enjoying and that I had the privilege of smelling as we ate
simultaneously. During this meal, I was to feign disinterest at
their food and pretend to be fully satisfied with my canned or dry
dog food. I was never able to fully master this final expectation.

Because Mom had never owned a dog before me during her
adult life, she was a bit squeamish at first about some things
involved in dog stewardship. For one thing, at first she wasn't
particularly fond of my wet tongue on her face. This made it a bit
of a challenge for me to kiss her whenever I suddenly had an urge
to. Also, at the touch of the velvety moistness of my cold nose on
her hands, she would quickly wipe away the spot. I noticed that
Mom was constantly wiping the surfaces of their many household
possessions and furnishings whenever my nose had made contact
with them. And then there were the excess personal items that I
helped them get rid of, as when I'd helped free Doug of his. They
were good sports through most of it. Eventually, Mom resisted
the impulse to immediately grab the vacuum to clean up the
trail of furry tufts I often left behind and grew to accept it like
Dad did. Even the nose prints I made were left until the usual
weekly housecleaning. I was glad then because I felt that those
nose prints were my own personal artwork, and the house was my
gallery. I even discovered that a clean sliding glass door makes
an excellent canvas. I sometimes have heard Mom and Dad talk
about those early times when I first came into their lives with

fondness and humor. I remember when they began to love me as much as I already loved them. My arrival had changed their lives in a positive way, and I know they felt the same as me—that what we had together was a very good thing indeed.

As a puppy toddler, I had my secret trespasses, and I became highly skilled at hiding my transgressions from my folks. Getting down off the furniture when I heard someone approaching was something for which I could thank my rapidly developing senses of smell and hearing. Using my nose, I would easily identify which parent was coming. Dad wasn't terribly finicky about the furniture, so I wouldn't bother to disembark if he was the one entering the room. I was rarely caught by Mom in the act, and if not for the residual fur I'd left behind, she wouldn't have known at all. Initially, I wasn't allowed in the bedroom especially during the early months of our cohabitation. I later came to understand that Mom suffers from seasonal allergies, which can be intense under certain circumstances. It seems that my presence, coupled with the fact that I was going through a seasonal shedding period, exacerbated her condition, and the bedroom was her only refuge. Although she never said so, I'm also convinced it probably also had something to do with my perpetual wet-nosing of everything, my slight dog odor, and the occasional accident I had, which was extremely rare. Over time, that squeamishness lessened; and the day did finally come when my dog odor, which was a natural thing in spite of my folk's continual bathing of me, ceased to be noticeable or bothersome to Mom. I stopped having accidents after a while too. And once it was determined that my presence wasn't complicating her allergy and the tumbling tumbleweeds I left behind wherever I went could easily be vacuumed, I was allowed virtually full access to our home. This too came later.

Back then, when I was just a puppy, my desire to be with my people constantly didn't stop when bedtime came, so consequently I would spend hours crying at their bedroom door, begging to sleep with them, as I had grown used to doing with Doug and little Sara. Eventually giving in to my own tiredness, I'd curl up against the door and fall asleep in a heap, exhausted. Dad would always be the first to appear the next day and would take me out for my morning *constitutional*. In my delight at the sight of him, I'd forget the rejection of the previous night, and all would be forgiven as we'd sit together and wait with rapt anticipation for Mom to come out of the bedroom. When she did appear, I'd go into full friendly attack mode skidding several feet to a halt at her feet on the vinyl tile floor. Actually, I often crashed right into her legs when I couldn't stop my skidding in time, but she would just laugh. My joy and enthusiasm at seeing her was always met with a big hug and lots of attention. Then she would pick me up and carry me back into the living room, something she's not been able to do for many years as I've grown quite large since then. I'd also quickly forgive her for making me sleep alone, and then I'd keep her slippered feet warm with my chin while she had her morning coffee.

It didn't take long for me to realize that I had an uncanny ability to get favors and attention from my parents more easily by using a staring technique, which I've been able to master over the years. Even though I was extremely happy in my life with them and had no serious complaints, I was born with a perpetually sad expression on my face and a peculiar countenance about me that drew the sympathy of those who looked upon me. The self-awareness of my lovely sad eyes and why I was able to manipulate my parents with them came about by accident. One day, when Mom and Dad weren't home and had inadvertently left the bedroom door ajar, I entered the forbidden territory intending to see firsthand what it was that I was being denied. Excited at my escapade, I was running around and pressing my wet nose against every piece of furniture I could find when I happened to pass the full length mirror that hung on the inside of the door. Thinking I'd caught a glimpse of another animal in my peripheral vision, I was surprised and alarmed since I'd not picked up an identifying scent to warn me of a possible territorial encroachment. I approached the mirror cautiously to take a closer look. I was stunned when I came face to face with my birth mom who stared back at me. I immediately wondered how she was able to find me after all that time. She appeared to be smaller than I'd remembered too. However, as the image mimicked my exact movements, I began to realize it was my own reflection! Besides being taken aback in initial disbelief at how much I looked like my birth mom, I was shocked by the sadness of my black outlined eyes and almost got caught up in self-pity at the sight of them.

The deplorable hardship I'd endured in my early life clearly left its mark in the profound sadness expressed in those eyes that stared back at me that day. Even though my existence had taken a complete reversal of fortune and my prospects had no bounds, my eyes would forever exude sorrow, even when I was experiencing sheer joy. In addition, it was on that day in front of the mirror that I realized for the first time that I wasn't half bad to look at either, and it did wonders for my self-esteem. The sight of my rusty red and white coat, the long mane around my neck and hind end, the bushy curved-up tail, and freckles on my legs were all attributes I admired, and I took great care in examining each one. I was quite Collie-like, as had been my birth mom. The only difference I could tell was that her eyes hadn't been black rimmed, and her nose was brown unlike mine, which was pure black. I'd seen window reflections of myself, but until that day, I had assumed my color was more muted in nature.

Reluctantly, I left the bedroom when I heard the car pull into the drive, but the experience left an impression that stayed with me for weeks. I tried unsuccessfully for days after that to sneak back to the mirror, but the nose prints I'd left behind gave my adventure away, and Mom took extra care to always keep the door closed. Within a few months after that, I was given full access to the bedroom; but the time came when my mirror image no longer held any fascination for me, especially once I was able to figure out the mirror's reflective properties.

I have to confess that over the years, I've shamefully used my beautiful soulful eyes to my benefit at every opportunity. Because Mom is so blindly in love with me, she's fallen for it almost every time. If I were a betting dog, I could have made a fortune on the pure certainty of being able to sucker her into anything I've wanted. I wish I could tell both parents that my love for them was never conditioned on handouts though, because I would have loved my people unconditionally even if I wasn't the most spoiled dog on the planet.

Through the Woods and Beyond

A dog has the soul of a philosopher.

—Plato

The yard where I live, here in Massachusetts with my forever family, has ample room to run but is located near a heavy traffic area. For this reason, I was rarely allowed off the leash. As I grew into maturity, I was allowed to walk without the leash alongside one of my parents but was always tethered to a shady tree when unattended. Our property has an expanse of woods on one side, and throughout my life, I've been taken for my walks through those woods along a worn path we've forged over the years. Although it's been more than a year since I've been on one of those trails because of my arthritis pain, I savor the memories of them and can still smell the forest floor in my mind if I think about it hard enough.

Some of my favorite walks, though, were taken on an adjacent piece of land on the other side of our woods. It's a large industrial property, beautifully maintained and surrounded on all sides by forest. Access to the factories and office buildings on the property is by way of a long winding scenic roadway that runs about a mile inland from the busy main road with a groomed sidewalk upon which our walks are mostly taken. The factory and office buildings are connected by a network of shady paved drives and pathways that run through groomed lawns and grass islands and lead from one building to another. Occasionally, we've gone off the sidewalk and into the woods where there are groomed jogging trails, footpaths, and a number of small wooden bridges that span the many small brooks and marshy areas throughout the property. The route we usually took along the inner perimeter of the complex covers about two miles, and walking there was always a real treat for me. A few years ago, we were temporarily denied access to this property by a new owner, but those restrictions were soon lifted, and we were once again allowed to walk there. These days, because I'm impaired by my physical limitations, I can only look over at the path through our woods that runs to that magnificent property. I'm pained by the fact that it's so near, yet I cannot go there. I miss it terribly...

When I first came to live here and was learning the art of walking with a leash, I usually wanted to go faster than humans were able to walk or even run. Sometimes on weekends, when the factories were closed and the parking lot was empty, I was allowed off the leash for a little bit, so I could run as fast as I wanted to. This, of course, was only after I could be trusted to stay with my family. Even then, it usually made Mom really nervous. I always stayed within sight of her—well, almost always. At least *I* could either see or smell her at all times, even though the reverse didn't hold true. I remember that as a puppy, I believed *I* was responsible for whoever was walking with me, not the reverse. If I was alone with Mom, I would be particularly alert for danger and ready for attack at any moment, having been trained by my birth mom on the art of intimidation. Fortunately, this was never necessary, and Mom and I always made it home safely. This is not to say we never had our share of problems.

On one really warm day, when I was still less than a year old, we were out on our daily walk. I was trotting along in front of Mom as she did a slow jog at my heels. I was suddenly distracted by something in the woods and abruptly stopped dead in my tracks, sending Mom toppling headfirst over me and into the pavement. Fortunately, she wasn't seriously hurt, but I could tell that it set kind of a bad tone for the rest of the walk. No longer jogging, she began limping; and thinking only of myself, I tugged at the leash, demanding that she keep pace with me in spite of her injury. Eventually, I became thirsty and tried to drag her through the woods, off trail so that I could drink from one of the many small brooks and streams that ran through the property. I'd tried this many times before that day but was never allowed to because Mom and Dad thought the iridescent film on the surface of the water indicated that it might have been polluted by spill from the factories. They usually had bottled water on them that they gave me in their cupped hand, but that day, Mom had used what was left in her water bottle to rinse the blood off her leg.

I became annoyed. As she tried to get me to continue on toward home and water, I pulled back on the leash, eventually sat down, and refused to go one step further. No amount of pleading or tugging from Mom could get me to budge. I was technically still a puppy, but I was at least halfway to what would be my full adult size, so her attempt to carry me proved to be too much for her. I stubbornly held my ground and resisted every attempt to move me. (This all took place at a time before cell phones were readily available.) Without any options, Mom sat down on the curb where she began to cry. As I looked upon my Mom who was crying her eyes out, I noticed for the first time that her knees and elbows were bleeding from the fall she'd taken. A surge of pity and compassion come over me. It was an emotion that was new to me. I got up off my haunches and walked over to her, kissed her face with my wet tongue, and attempted to tend to her wounds, but she wouldn't let me. That time, she didn't jerk away from the touch of my wet nose as she usually did. I think that our relationship made a major breakthrough that day. I had exhibited empathy toward something other than myself, and she had found that my kisses weren't so disgusting after all. I immediately stopped being stubborn and walked her home, pulling her along on my leash as she limped behind me.

On a rare occasion, to the horror of my parents, I would launch out of the house like a rocket the instant the front door was opened. It was usually due to the carelessness of a young grandchild or an unsuspecting house guest. Apparently, they hadn't been forewarned of the fact that I was a potential escapee just waiting for my opportunity to break free of household bondage and go on an unrestricted run. Temporarily untethered, I'd race up the path toward the factory property on the other side of our woods. Because I had the ability to run so fast, I would be out of sight in about thirty seconds flat and reach the factory property in less than a minute. They had no way of knowing this, but because they'd trained me so well, I always stayed on the sidewalks and jogging trails and never crossed the road. It was probably foolhardy of me at the time, but I did drink the forbidden water on those occasions. I knew I was going to be in trouble for my escape, and after burning off most of my pent up energy, I'd go back home with my head down, looking appropriately ashamed (although I never was). Within minutes, one or both of my parents would be on their way to meet me with a scornful expression and the retractable leash in hand. After a proper scolding, I could tell that they were far more relieved than angry.

Early in that first summer with my *forever* family, my parents began packing for a trip to their summer camp in Vermont. It's located on the crest of a ridge in the Green Mountain range, smack in the middle of a sixty-four acre tract. Sensing another dreaded car ride, I watched them preparing for days in the same way Doug had packed for the ill-fated Florida trip. Out of desperation, I plotted an escape route should they try to force me into the car. My thoughts of fleeing weren't realistic though, as I had no desire to escape from the parents that I adored or to return to my former life of continual upheaval and insecurity. It was out of my hands anyway as their plans had been made, and I was going with them. Out of panic, I did put up a formidable fight as they placed me into the back seat of Dad's pickup when the day finally came to leave.

My fear of road travel never left me as my early experience with Doug had forever tarnished that which is normally a dog's greatest thrill—to ride in a vehicle beside his or her people. Although I hated the three-hour drive in the back seat of the truck's cab, it was well worth it in the end, but I had no way of knowing that until after my first trip. I'd been given very little to eat at breakfast—something that had annoyed me a lot that morning, especially when my begging for more went ignored. I've come to understand that it is better for me to travel on a slightly empty stomach. On that first long trip, I had plenty of room in the back where Dad had put the back seat down, giving me a nice flat platform on which to lie down or sit comfortably. Even so, I shuddered and shook for the entire trip and covered everything around me with drool and fur. They kept the air conditioning on though, and in spite of my fear, I was fairly comfortable. Nevertheless, Mom and Dad calmly accepted this as one of my many quirks, being just the result of my unfortunate past. They never made me feel guilty about it.

My wildest imagination couldn't have prepared me for the awe I experienced when we reached the cabin high in the hills. I had never seen a view so breathtaking. I was released from the car when we'd reached the top of the long driveway, and I was allowed to go off and run to my heart's content, and burn off all vestiges of travel fatigue. The large expanse of land that was our designated property consists of clusters of softly rolling hills dotted with white pine, spruce, apple, and a variety of hardwoods. Patches of snow left over from winter were still quite prevalent due to the elevation of the cabin. This is normal for late May in Vermont I've come to realize. Every year it would take me by surprise, though, because in Massachusetts, the snow was usually gone for good by April.

As Mom and Dad unloaded the car, I raced from hill to hill amazed at how far into the distance I was able to see. I ran until my legs nearly buckled in exhaustion, and when I got overheated, I threw myself into the little pockets of leftover winter snow gathered in drifts at the base of the gigantic pine trees. It was only then that I took the time to notice that the air in Vermont had a fresh minty odor unlike that of Massachusetts, which was also pleasant but different. Over the years, now that my olfactory senses have been highly developed, I've noticed other scents that comprise the Vermont air in the spring including that of cow manure, which tends to be strong at first but will become less prevalent as the summer approaches. In every direction I turned, that first day in Vermont, I picked up scents that were unfamiliar but promising. I didn't quite understand it at the time, but my world had just been expanded, and there would be a plethora of wonderful discoveries to be made in my future. After I briefly rested and then rolled in the snow until I was cooled off, I ran some more. When I got thirsty, I ate some of the snow, a habit I'd acquired back at the old house when the dripping spigot was frozen. I could see Mom and Dad as they watched me from the sliding glass door. I knew they were awfully trusting to allow me to run free that day. When I showed up at the door to be let in, I sniffed and wet-nosed every part of the cabin's interior. After I drank about a gallon of water, I was once again allowed to go outside where I carefully marked my newly acquired territory.

I gave myself some serious shin splints that spring as a result of those first few days of excessive running. I continued to do this annually and suffered through temporary muscle and joint pain, which soon would be gone and forgotten within the week of arrival. Although I loved my walks in Massachusetts—even though I was usually restricted by a thirty-foot retractable leash—nothing could beat the thrill of freedom that I had in Vermont. There I could move about at my own pace and investigate to my heart's content the many things about nature, waiting to be discovered. I still yearn for Vermont. One of my deepest regrets is never seeing our place again as I know my death is close at hand. I'll not be making it back up there this year.

I realize that where I die is something I have no control over. It's been hardwired into me to accept my short life here on this earth, having served my purpose—to love and be loved. There is no fear in it. Wherever it is that I go, I'm hoping mostly for no more pain—for that alone, I'd be so grateful. I try hard not to think too much about the hereafter and get my hopes up too high, as I've heard Mom say that nothing is written in the Bible, God's book, regarding the afterlife of animals; but she's comforted in the fact that it doesn't specifically say that nothing happens, or that it's totally over for us forever.

We animals are very much aware of the existence of God. He's given us that revelation through his creation and instilled in us the survival instincts that we need for life. Other attributes such as love and care for our offspring and animal families and even sometimes other animals outside of our own species, clearly indicate a certain degree of intellect. Our displays of emotions that range from pure joy to utter sadness are obvious signs of the existence of our spiritual nature. God has even given us dogs the added ability to engage the human race on a more personal level than any other creature. Maybe the reason God didn't tell the humans more about us in the Bible was that he just wanted humans to listen to the special message he had for *them* and *their* relationship with him. Mom used to say that if God didn't tell us something in his book, that meant he had it covered, and we shouldn't worry about it. I personally hope that my spirit will be going someplace after I pass from this earth. Maybe there's a paradise just for the animal world. One that smells like the

Vermont hills with lots of fresh grass. I overheard Mom talking about whether or not God has made provision for animals after death, such as providing them with a heavenly domain. "After all," she said, "animals weren't the ones that sinned in the garden of Eden." If there is such a place, I plan on looking for my birth mom as soon as I get there, because now, knowing what I know about life, she surely would deserve to go there when she died.

From the beginning of my life with my forever family, I was meant to be primarily Mom's canine companion and body guard, though I was generously included in both Mom's and Dad's leisure activities when they were home. When at the cabin, our leisure activities included hiking on our sixty-four acres of land. During my first summer, we travelled almost every weekend back to the house in Massachusetts to replenish supplies until the Vermont cabin was completed. In subsequent years, we stayed in Vermont for whole months at a time. Probably my fondest memories are of those times we spent up there since, for the most part, I was usually off-leash and had far more opportunities than our home here in Massachusetts could have afforded me. Mom and Dad were different in Vermont too. More relaxed and also more willing to go along with me when I tried to engage them in a yard game that included running or chasing. Back then, I'd sometimes spot Mom peacefully strolling along the outer perimeter of the yard or sneaking down the driveway for one of her road walks, trying to avoid catching my eye, so I wouldn't follow her. Her ignorance, as she was slinking away, was in thinking it was my vision that betrayed her presence when, as with all dogs, it was my nose that was the first responder of all my senses. Usually keeping myself positioned downwind of people whenever possible, I was keenly aware of their whereabouts at any given moment. Because of this, I was rarely taken by surprise unless crept up upon as I slept.

Consequently, trying to slip off unnoticed was an act of futility on Mom's part.

Although Mom did like to take the occasional walk alone that didn't include being hindered by my antics and demands on her, she was seldom allowed by me to do so. As always was the case, I would be thrilled to see Mom setting out for her walk, headset on and chugging along at an energetic pace. I'd run over to join her, and in my excitement, I'd try to entice her into a game of Tag or Tug of War with my wet deflated football. Apparently, she didn't share my enthusiasm for these games, yet I didn't care, and I'd poke her continually with the ball as she walked and tried to ignore me. Unwilling to be rebuffed, I'd drop the ball and poke her directly with my wet nose against her legs, begging her for a response; but usually she'd just continue on, ignoring me. Not willing to give up entirely, I'd accept that she didn't want to play. I'd settle for being a silent companion, and quietly, I'd follow closely behind her. At those times, just being near her was enough to satisfy me. As I matured, I too came to enjoy having my own space sometimes just to be alone in my canine musings. I have heard Mom say recently that she regrets not having been more willing to come out and play with me while I was still physically able to play. I wish she didn't feel guilty about that because the truth is she did, in fact, spend a lot of quality time with me back then. I'll never forget all the times over the years when Mom and I were practically joined at the hip for whole days on end. We'd often sit on our favorite grassy knoll and soak in the magnificent views below. I'd sit in front of her, and she'd give me a shoulder massage and a head scratch as we looked out at the breathtaking vista below us. At those times, Mom would often pray aloud but softly to herself, and I sometimes even heard my name mentioned. I remember once I heard her thanking God for bringing me into her and Dad's life like he did. After I thought I'd allowed her ample time to sit there and meditate, I'd beg her to get up and chase me, and she usually did!

I suppose I must have been a pest at times back when I was inclined to be quite needy, and I erroneously thought that everything was about me and for me. As far as I was concerned, no amount of play or attention from my parents was enough. During our first couple of summers in Vermont, their days working on the cabin and gardens were really too busy to satisfy my yearning to be the center of their universe. I remember I was always trying to push my wet and slimy deflated football into anyone's hand, pleading with them to play with me. My deflated football, my most highly prized possession, was often coveted by the neighborhood dogs and visiting children. Realizing the appeal it held to others, despite its perpetual saliva-drenched condition, I always kept it within my reach; and I was seldom seen without it, even when sleeping. When it was first given to me, it was inflated and as such was a source of frustration for me as I was unable to firmly plant my jaws around it and carry it. After I accidentally punctured it with my teeth, it deflated. That turned out to be advantageous as I was then able to easily carry it wherever I went, and it also became easier to chew. Frankly, I never did understand why it was originally pumped full of air. Mom and Dad were still able to throw it as before, and I could get a good grip on it for Tug of War. I was given a lot of play time, but it was never enough in my opinion; so I would pester my folks until they'd relent, drop what they were doing, and throw the ball for me to chase. My skills at the game of Fetch were limited though, and they'd soon grow tired of throwing the ball—which I would retrieve but would refuse to give back to them. Instead, I would try to get them to chase me for it. When and if they could catch me, I'd make them wrestle the ball out of my clenched jaw, which Mom was too weak to do. They quickly got tired of my refusal to play the game on their terms, and they'd go back to whatever task I'd interrupted. I was never able to fully train them in my version of Fetch, and after a few years, I gave up entirely in this pursuit.

Unfortunately, the day came when my beloved deflated football went missing. Although we searched high and low for weeks, it remained lost. It was suggested that maybe one of the neighborhood dogs borrowed it and had simply forgotten to return it. This was never proven to be the case but was never ruled out either. I was able to enjoy the ball for most of my life, though, and eventually, I lost the ability to run and chase after it anyway due to arthritis, which now plagues me. My lost ball was replaced by a smaller, bright orange vinyl one that never deflated in spite of my desperate efforts to flatten it, which initially infuriated me. On the positive side, it reminded me of the pink one Doug had bought me a long time before and which was among the toys I'd left behind. Even though the orange ball, and its reluctance to deflate, never made up for the loss of my missing leather football; it was much smaller, being a child's toy, and I could easily grasp it in my jaws when it was thrown to me.

When I was in my first year with Mom and Dad, my baby teeth were bothering me. I found relief from that gnawing itchy sensation they gave me by chewing on soft leathery things. This was the reason I was provided with the football in the first place. Shoes and purses had to be tucked away safely out of my sight; although later, a pair of Mom's boots met with an unfortunate ending. When I was teething, human skin had the consistency of leather to me, so I adopted an annoying habit of play-biting any human hand that attempted to pet me. My persistence in play-biting was met with a loud "No Bite!" from Mom, but my urge to chew, in combination with my constant desire to play, was strong, and I just couldn't help myself. My jaws weren't terribly strong at that stage of puppyhood, and my little teeth weren't capable of breaking the skin or drawing blood, but they did have the potential to scratch and cause some degree of pain to my victim. Each time someone would try to pet me, I believed it was a signal that they wanted to play a game of Bite. Finally, Dad began placing my paw into my own mouth, so my self-inflicted bites would help me to understand I was causing pain. My habit was soon broken. As far as Mom's favorite leather boots were concerned though, as Dad said at the time, she probably shouldn't have left them where she knew I would have access to them, and we both know he was right.

Food Beggar

If you find honey, eat just enough—too much of it, and you will vomit.

Proverbs 25:16 (NIV)

Never trust a dog to watch your food.

—Unknown

Out of compassion and convenience, I was always fed at the same time that my folks sat down to their meals. At my first veterinary appointment, it was recommended that I be immediately switched over to puppy chow—at least for the first two years. This was a difficult period for me because I'd already, by then, grown accustomed to adult dog food and some table scraps. I guess I did eventually get used to the puppy chow and even liked it. It was kept in a bowl by the door and always available to me, but I usually wasn't that interested in it until evening, at which time I'd wolf down the whole bowl. All my life, I've continued to ignore my bowl of dry kibble until the dinner dishes are done, and the kitchen is closed for the evening. Only then have I even considered eating my dry food. By the time I was two, I was ready to expand to more variety, and that's about the time when Mom's resolve not to give me table scraps began to unravel. It wasn't long before my desire for people food reestablished itself. At meal time, my food was quickly wolfed down in order that I might take my regular position under the dining table and beg for more. The table scraps were scraped into my bowl when the table was cleared, and oh, how I relished that moment! Unfortunately, this was probably not a good tradition to have started back then because the anticipation of this regular treat left me with a taste for homecooked people food—one of the thorns Mom would have to bear for the rest of my life, as I went on to become a hardcore food beggar.

I was always available to help in the kitchen, should they need it when a meal was being prepared. I strategically positioned myself where I'd be constantly underfoot and where ignoring me could prove to be hazardous. It was just my way of reminding them that I was not to be forgotten, and they should prepare enough for me of whatever it was they were cooking. Being careful where they stepped, they somehow managed to avoid stepping on my stretched-out body, which I flattened so as to spread myself out into as large an obstacle as I could possibly manage, lest they not notice me down there. In the meantime, the smell would drive me crazy; and I'd give Mom that pleading stare, which would ultimately result in my receiving a handout.

When I was about two years old, my family began growing their own corn. They plowed a small section of a field near the cabin not far from Mom's kitchen garden. It was a labor intensive activity, particularly the first year when the sod had to be turned over. Enduring the nagging buzz and stinging from a seasonal black fly onslaught, they threw themselves into the project until it was done. I watched in curiosity as the small holes were made with a stick and the individual kernels planted. To ensure the security and protection of the crop, an electric fence was installed around its circumference. I was shocked by its power only once, however, and I soon realized I could easily crawl under it as did many small nocturnal animals. Eventually through the summer, the field produced an immense quantity of tall stalks, the meaning of which initially eluded me (but only the first year). Later that summer, large pods grew from the tops of the stalks with curious-looking silky tops. Then Mom or Dad harvested the pods daily just before dinner. For the next couple of weeks, every afternoon one of them would gather enough of what they called *ears* (although I failed to see the resemblance to mine or theirs), and they would sit on the deck and peel away the layers, exposing a yellow interior covered in fine silky fibers. Although I'd seen Mom and Dad consume this food from time to time, I'd never been given any. Its odor after it was cooked seemed bland anyway, so I never begged for any either.

One night, during corn season, I watched as a family of raccoons raided the cornfield. It was one of the many occasions when Mom was calling me, and I was ignoring her, which was often my customary response if I understood it to mean I was being summoned indoors on a lovely cool evening. I noticed how the raccoons chewed the bottom of the stem, bent the stalk down, and tore off the ear of corn. I watched intently as they peeled off the husk with their pointy little teeth and then ate the yellow kernels off the cob inside. It was similar to the method used by my parents except that the raccoons ate with rapidity, their beady eyes looking nervously over their shoulders, trying to eat as much as they could before they got caught. They'd usually end up devouring a dozen or so ears before they were done. One afternoon after that, feeling bored and hungry, I was thinking about going inside to ask Mom for a Milk-Bone with peanut butter on it, one of my favorite afternoon snacks. Suddenly, I remembered the raccoons and ran down to the corn field, tore off an ear of corn, ran back up to the yard, husked it, and systematically cleaned it of every kernel. Picked fresh from the field and husked, it gave off a wonderful grassy scent, and I was surprised by the succulent sweetness of the kernels within. I began helping myself to an ear of corn directly from the field from time to time to the amusement of my parents. After that, Mom always made an extra ear of corn for me when it was on the night's menu. Following a few disappointing harvest years, they stopped growing their own, deeming it to be not worth the time and effort. It continued to be a summertime favorite though, and I was always included in the head count when they considered how much corn to buy from the market.

My craving for tasty food led me to sample a large variety of that which nature has to offer in the wild. When I was occasionally able to slip away from the eagle eye of my Mom, I took to sampling this bounty. I've tried mice, insects, snakes, rotting carcasses of various wild animals that didn't make it through the ravages of winter and basically anything that looked the slightest bit edible and tantalized my taste buds. I suppose I was never hungry enough to go beyond just small samplings, and that may have kept me from getting really sick. One day in early summer, I followed a scent trail that led me to a rotting deer carcass. With little resistance, the leg tore away easily from the aging deer corpse, and I determined to bring my prize home to add to my collection of buried treasures. This was a boneyard of leftovers from treats I'd been given but wasn't hungry enough to finish at the time they were given to me. I could see in my peripheral vision the lower part of the limb onto which the hoof was attached dangling up and down from the ankle joint as I trotted proudly up the drive. As it turned out, Dad wasn't happy with my trophy, and Mom was appalled. Not wanting me to "… become accustomed to the taste of fresh animal blood," as he put it, Dad tossed the deer leg into the bed of the old dump truck he kept far from the house. I can honestly attest, from my own observations of the crime scene, there wasn't any *fresh* blood to speak of on the ancient rotten corpse. I was extremely frustrated and annoyed at Dad's failure to accept my explanation of this as I whined and begged him to give the treasured leg back to me. I fretted for days, frustrated at my inability to access the deer leg, and I circled the dump truck over and over. I could still smell the leg, yet I couldn't retrieve it, so eventually, I gave up. I remembered the deer leg whenever I was around the area of the old dump truck over the next few years, but since there was nothing I could do to get it out, I didn't dwell on it. I'm sure the leg must have still been there when Dad eventually sold that truck, which had been out of service for a long time and was no longer needed at the cabin.

I can remember one time when I underwent severe digestive tract distress as a result of poisoning. I spent most of the following twenty-four hour period retching non-stop off the back deck and wishing I was dead. I was almost two years old at the time. Many guesses were voiced that day as to what could have been the cause, such as antifreeze from someone's driveway, wild mushrooms, poisonous insects, or a decaying bacteria-laden carcass. It definitely wasn't the latter because bacteria had never really had that much of an ill effect on me. I'm certain the filth of my early puppyhood under the porch of my birth mom's old house had given me immunity from bacteria strains yet to be discovered by human science. Being a Sunday, the animal clinic was closed, so my desperate parents got in touch with the veterinarian on call at his home. After hearing the symptoms, he concluded that I would probably be okay, but he told them to call him back if I failed to show significant improvement by the next day. Accusations were loudly thrown between my folks that day although no blame was cast since they had both failed to ensure that I didn't escape again. I was frustrated by the fact that I knew what made me ill yet was unable to communicate that reason to them.

What happened was, after sneaking off from time to time and making a nuisance of myself at the home of a distant neighbor that summer, I regularly ignored his gruff shouts to "Get out of here!" I'm sure he was suspicious of the interest I showed in the sheep he kept. If I'd been given half the chance, I may have even been inclined to chase them, as I have to admit at the time I was leaning in that direction. However, on my few visits there, I was never able to find the sheep alone for very long as my sudden appearance would stir them into a frenzy of bleating, and their human protector would suddenly appear to defend them from me. On that particular morning, he'd made me his first ever food offering. Actually, it was a blood offering—raw ground beef, which I found to be quite enticing in spite of the fact that it smelled a little *off* but not bad enough to bother me. In the spirit of youthful, blind trust, I accepted the treat without questioning his sudden friendliness—an attitude change that should have sent up a red flag. Back at home later, as I was heaving off of the back deck for the umpteenth time, I suddenly remembered and realized the deception of the neighbor. Now I was paying the price for my gullibility. No doubt, the fake peace offering had been poisoned. I don't believe he intended to kill me though, and I'd like to think that he just wanted to send me a message. Fortunately, I was able to vomit out the vast majority of whatever the neighbor poisoned me with. To my disappointment, I was not allowed out of Mom's sight, *and* I was put on a bland diet for at least a week.

A few weeks after the poisoning, I managed to escape for a short period of time from my watchful parents; and I decided to pay a courtesy call to the neighbor, although I didn't cross under the barbed wire which served as the boundary of his property. He seemed surprised and disappointed to see me alive and well. His reaction amused me considerably, but I had gotten his message that he didn't want me hanging around his land or his sheep. Since that time, I've avoided that property. Also after that, I was usually much more careful about accepting food gifts from perfect strangers, unless my parents were around. My eventual graduation to adult dog food by the time I turned two helped to appease my more mature palate, and I naturally became less inclined to taste test every unusual thing that came into my path.

Raspberries and blackberries grew abundantly on our land. I learned on my own to identify the ripeness by the color. I'm almost certain I would have loved the fruit pies Mom sometimes made with them, but since they were much coveted by the humans, I was never offered any. Strangely, although I always searched, the pie never seemed to be included in the table scraps I was given. My sweet tooth didn't stop with fruit, and I've always loved any sort of pastry or sugary foods. Often, I've been pleasantly surprised when I'm given a scoop of vanilla ice cream if it's on the menu for dessert.

Now that I'm old, thinking of all the food I've had and loved over the years makes me almost wish I had my appetite back, but I know I'd just heave them back up if I tried. It's nice to just lie here and think about them though. In her worry over me lately, Mom's been offering me some of my old favorites. I'm just not interested in eating very much these past few days. A couple of weeks ago, she even started buying the little gourmet food pouches that are formulated for the lighter digestive constitution of small dogs. Actually, they weren't bad but seemed a little on the bland side for my tastes.

One time when Mom and Dad were away in Florida and I was staying at Ken and Brooke's house, they were hosting a party and invited several friends. My jaw dropped when I saw the snack tray Brooke set out on the coffee table, and the drool started streaming from my open mouth nonstop. The tray was filled with cheese, salami, crackers, chips and sour cream dip, tortilla chips, and little hotdogs in barbeque sauce. Although I never had access to those foods at home, I could tell by the way they smelled that they were things I would love to taste test! We dogs watched from the vantage point of the kitchen, as we were not allowed into the living room for the party. Evidently, Brooke didn't realize that although her own dogs were trustworthy, I wasn't yet coffee table trained. When the guests and hosts stepped out onto the porch for some fresh evening air, I took the initiative of entering the forbidden living room to help myself to what I assumed were the table scraps I would normally have been entitled to (although not in so great a quantity) if I were home with my parents. I wolfed down as much as I could as I knew that time was short, and the humans would be back inside soon. I also ignored all the warnings from Champ and Sadie (a Siberian Husky mix and their newest adoptee) as they both whined nervously and backed out of the room, staying as far away from me and the crime scene as possible. When the party came back into the house ten minutes later, Brooke wasn't appreciative of my having helped myself (without waiting to be served, I guessed at the time). But she was a compassionate and kind woman, taking into consideration that missing Mom and Dad had most likely caused my temporary lapse in judgment, and my breach was quickly forgiven. The fact of the matter was that I wasn't used to their stringently adhered to no-table-scrap rule, which was unheard of at our house. Nevertheless, I'd consumed an unusually large and spicy serving of food that I wasn't accustomed to, and I didn't feel well for a couple of days after that. Champ seemed a little too smug at my distress, and my guess is, judging from the twinkle in his eye, that if he'd been more vocal, he would have had something clever to say.

I never did get used to that no-table-scrap rule at Ken's. I remember watching in horror at the sight of chicken nuggets, spaghetti and meatballs, or turkey with gravy as they were being scraped from the kid's plates into the garbage can, and I'd have to avert my eyes to be able to bear it! Naturally, the garbage can had to be kept behind the closed basement door when I was visiting their household. I just wasn't used to living in a household where human children were in residence, and I missed being given the special attention that was normally bestowed on me by Mom and

Dad as though I was an only child. When my folks did bring me back home, it didn't take them long to reprogram me.

Remembering the snack tray incident at Ken's reminds me of how much I'm going to miss them! It was really nice of Ken to stop by this morning just to check up on how I was doing. He seemed so sad when he said "Bye, Jessie!" I'm sure he knows he won't be seeing me again, and he knows how my parents will feel after I'm gone because Champ died last year. It's good to know Ken will be there to help them through the mourning process. I had a hard time staying awake during his visit though. When I woke up from my nap, I looked out through the sliding glass door, and I saw him digging a hole under my shade tree with his tractor. I wonder what that's for. Maybe when Mom and Dad carry me outside for my *business* later, they'll take me over there so that I can get a good look at it.

As a fully mature dog, I rarely ate things I shouldn't have; but I was always curious about chocolate, a food that smelled good to me, but I was not allowed access to. Once on Christmas day, I noticed a bowl of candy on the coffee table, and I could easily smell the chocolate through the hard shell coating on every piece. It was the entire contents of a large value-sized bag in holiday colors, which is probably what attracted me to them in the first place. Mom was busy vacuuming and cleaning in the living room in preparation for our annual family party while I moved from room to room to escape the dreaded vacuum cleaner. She wasn't concerned since by then, I was pretty much coffee table trained; but that day, I apparently had a temporary lapse in judgment. I remember Dad always told the grandchildren not to give me chocolate if they were eating any since it was toxic to dogs. I had no desire to be poisoned, as I'd never really gotten over the sheep farmer incident and remembered the word *poison* was mentioned repeatedly during that time. Yet the smell of the candy in the bowl that day overpowered any self-control I had, and I devoured all of it, licking the bowl clean. Not too long after the empty bowl was discovered, my parents noticed that I looked sick. In fact, I felt terrible! Jumping into action, Dad took me out on my retractable leash to the back yard where I vomited chocolate for about ten full minutes. As I heaved, I marveled that something that tasted so good could cause so much misery. Since it was Christmas Day, of course the vet wouldn't be available. It was determined that I'd eliminated most of the bag's contents, and what remained in my stomach probably wasn't a lethal dose of chocolate for my weight. I was closely watched for the rest of the night, although Mom and Dad were on the verge of taking me to the Boston emergency animal hospital if things got worse. They were relieved when I lived to see another day, and I was back to my old self a few days later. The only downside to all this was that because of my mischief, I was left with no appetite for the leftovers, which could have been mine after the Christmas feast.

Off My Leash

We are driven by five genetic needs; survival, love and belonging, power, freedom, and fun.

—William Glasser

By the time I was several years old, I was considered to be somewhat trustworthy, and whenever we were in Vermont, I'd spend a large portion of the day exploring our sixty-four acres. Our land was part of the original farm tract that previously belonged to Dad's older sister and was later subdivided into five tracts and sold off, one portion being our property. Mom was constantly in search of me, as Dad insisted I not be confined on a dog run, as was required in Massachusetts. Back then in Vermont, unless pets were a nuisance to the neighbors, there was no leash law in the rural areas of our town, and dogs could roam freely. I did take Mom with me on many of those expeditions of mine, but she always slowed me down, and I'd get impatient always waiting for her to catch up. After I grew tired of dragging her along behind me, I'd take off on my own and never felt guilty when I heard Mom calling and calling, and I'd usually get back to the cabin before her. I knew my way around our property though, and my water bucket, which Dad kept full of ice cold well water, always beckoned me home at regular intervals throughout the day. I was free to be in the house anytime I wanted to and had full access to every room, once I'd reached the age of two.

For the first few summers of my life, we traveled back and forth between Vermont and Massachusetts almost weekly until the cabin was ready for more permanent seasonal habitation. I remember its completion was a great relief to me because it meant fewer road trips, and I could take the time to explore once I was given a little more freedom to roam around our property. I had a few private places where I would enjoy quiet time and an occasional nap in the shade. I didn't like being in the direct sun for my nap. My coat of red and white was quite thick, and I had a Collie's mane around my neck. The rest of me was shorter haired yet thick enough to make me uncomfortably warm in the heat. Under the deck of the cabin, there was a crawl space—an area that closely resembled the dimensions of my birth home—where I used to enjoy resting on hot, sultry days. It also served to afford me some privacy when we had company. Considering the squalor of my early life under the porch of my birth mom's house, it astounds me that I would ever be compelled to go below a deck of any kind but the heat drove me to do just that. Unlike the old house, though, it was cool and pleasant below our cabin's deck in Vermont. The fresh, clean smell of the loam Dad's tractor had spread against the foundation was far superior to the grimy muck my birth family and I had lived in, and that had probably included our own waste. Once I discovered how pleasant it was below our deck in Vermont, I did some excavation down there, forming a well in the dirt, which was just my size and shape. It provided a cozy but cool bed for me on the hottest days. The soft loam made an excellent site for the boneyard I started when I buried some soup bones. Until that lair of mine was discovered by my folks, I could spend an hour here and there in peaceful repose while they were frantically looking for me and calling my name over and over. Oblivious to their concern and reluctant to leave the cool comfort of my bed of soil, I blissfully ignored their calls. When I was finally ready to reemerge, I would sneak out of my secret place, lest it be discovered. After I saw the extreme relief upon their faces at my reappearance, I should have been ashamed of myself for keeping this from them, but I never was. Eventually though, I was actually seen emerging from under the deck; and after that, if I went missing, it was the first place where my parents looked.

One hot summer day, I was locked in the house as Mom and Dad were out doing errands. They always left the door to the downstairs open so that I could retreat to the cooler basement level if I wanted. After snooping around looking for a spot down there to escape the heat, I discovered the store room, its door inadvertently left ajar. I went in to investigate the new territory in a house that I had mistakenly thought I knew from top to bottom. The temperature in the small room was more conducive to my comfort requirements. After sometimes finding me lying on the cool cement floor of that closet, Mom and Dad finally realized that it was one of my favorite hideaways, and its door was always left ajar for my convenience. Only Mom and Dad knew about my hiding places, and they never betrayed my confidence. Those secret places sheltered me from the ravages of the summer heat, lightning storms, and the roughhousing of unruly children who belonged to occasional houseguests.

If we had an extended rainy stretch that produced puddles, I delighted in finding the muddiest of these to soak my lush coat to the skin. This got Mom and Dad thinking, and being tired of bathing me daily upon my return in a sorry state of muck, they bought a child's wading pool for me. Dad heard of other dogs that enjoyed cooling off in children's wading pools. It was filled lovingly with half ice cold well water from the hose and half with hot water from the kitchen tap, which Mom laboriously carried pail by pail out the back door and down the stairs to the pool, bringing the water temperature to a comfortable seventy degrees. I know I hurt their feelings when their efforts were rewarded with total indifference and lack of enthusiasm on my part. It just wasn't the same as my puddles, and I actually preferred the mud bath in the drainage ditch over this pristine plastic pool, which smelled like the petroleum product it was. The wading pool sat unused in the yard for the remainder of the season that year. Even the young children of visiting guests took little interest in it, and ultimately, it was quietly packed away in September and sold at a neighbor's garage sale the following year. The patch of dead grass where the pool had sat for an entire season eventually grew back and became one of my favorite places to take an afternoon siesta after the sun had made its way to the other side of the house.

I've been somewhat confused these past few months of my infirmity due to old age. A strange incident happened during the night recently. I'm guessing it's probably the beginning of the end for me. I was walking in my sleep, and for some strange reason, I thought I was standing in a pool of water. It made me feel like I had to relieve myself. Not wanting to wake up Dad to take me out to my bush, I decided to just *go* in the water I thought I was standing in. I was really surprised when I suddenly woke up, and I was actually standing in the middle of the room, and I couldn't stop the flow. I believe the incident was just an anomaly, but after it happened, Mom started getting up to take me outside in the middle of the night using that ramp I've come to hate. I was uncooperative about going out these past two nights, but she didn't force the issue, and I managed to stay dry till morning.

Mom has a habit of singing to me while she performs tasks around the house. They're made-up lyrics that are about me, and she sings them to the tune of old television commercials, shows, or even nursery rhymes. Usually making the words up as she goes along, she uses catchy phrases that are easily memorized for future use. Over the course of my life, Mom has acquired a significant repertoire to choose from if she's in the mood, and I'm around to listen. I just love hearing them, though Dad thinks they're dumb, and he refuses to sing along. One of my favorites (in fact she still sings it to me every day) is sung to the tune of a popular Christmastime favorite, "It's the Most Wonderful Time of the Year." I still hear Mom's voice in my head—like an ear worm—as she sings the words "She's the most wonderful dog in the world. Her name is Jessie, and she's part of our family, and we love her soooo! She's the most wonderful dog in the world."

There were other great songs she made up about me, but I really don't want to think about them now because it only makes me sad. I know she's just trying to cheer me up though.

When we are at the summer cabin in Vermont, we often have company visit on the weekends. I look forward to this as a welcome diversion. In the past, my awareness of the imminent arrival of guests was usually due to certain clues I'd pick up on such as the preparations that would take place outside of Mom's normal routine. For instance, my food and water bowl would be moved to a different location out of the path of foot traffic, and I would be given a bath. Dusting and vacuuming (which I hated) would take place in the guest section of the cabin, which was an area usually left undisturbed behind closed doors. If the names mentioned by Mom or Dad were unfamiliar to me, I never stressed over who to expect, whether I knew them or not, whether they would bring other dogs with them, or if they would be bringing children. I just waited patiently until they arrived and accepted each group on their own merits as I had no choice in the matter anyway. Many of them were repeat guests, so I did sometimes have some preconceived idea of how the weekend would transpire. I was often taken aback on how much children I *thought* I knew would change in appearance and personality in the one year's time since I'd last seen them. There were times I'd fully expect and look forward to a playful child who had doted on me during the previous summer's visit only to be confronted on their next visit, a year later, by a sullen preteen who was an imposter of the former child and who no longer showed interest in me—even to the point of seeming to have no recollection of ever having known me! It never occurred to me that my presence would be a nuisance to anyone and probably shouldn't have been concerned one way or the other if it was. This was, after all, my home, and they were the intruders. For my own self-esteem, though, I needed acceptance from most humans; and if I sensed disinterest or disdain, I would set out to force them to like me.

This was the case with Dad's elderly sister, Priscilla, the former owner of our land. She was one of the guests who visited us annually, but unlike the others, she abruptly rejected my offer of friendship when I approached her car and put my wet nose in her hand. For some reason that I've never understood, that gesture caused her to suddenly yank her arm away in disgust. Her stubborn, continued resistance to my advances throughout the weekend only served to make me try even harder to break through the resolve she had to avoid any contact with me. Normally, as was the case with other people, my persistence produced a certain level of resignation from my target person, and they'd try to appease me with a cursory pat or two on the head. Some folks, as in Priscilla's case, were just plain dog-a-phobic and hard to get through to. I finally gave up in defeat that weekend, but I refused to give up totally in my resolve to earn Priscilla's approval; and I continued for years, unsuccessfully, to try and break down the invisible wall that divided us.

Never lacking for affection from Mom and Dad, I still enjoyed the initial attention from the regulars who came every year, who liked me a lot and lavished me with loving embraces upon their arrival. Then I was content to stay out of the way, especially as my arthritic years began. I just loved watching from a short distance, or listening from the safety of my nest below the deck, to the soft chatter and clinking of glasses, and basking in the knowledge that a special dinner would be ensuing, along with those much looked forward to after-dinner leftovers, which were due me for my good behavior.

Normally when I was locked inside while Mom and Dad went out on errands, I hated it even though it rarely went beyond a few hours. On weekends when we had visiting guests, though, I was locked inside so that they and their company could go to lunch and tourist destinations, and the absences tended to be longer than their typical errands. I would become incredibly bored. To remedy this, being careful not to leave any signs such as drool or shedding hair, I'd use up the time investigating and looking for clues in the guest bedrooms that might help me know them better. I'd look around, pressing my nose against everything not carefully stowed away in their suitcases. I'd take an interest in whatever belongings they had laying about, particularly noting the different smells, sometimes finding food items and partaking of them. I was able to learn an awful lot from the scents I picked up on their personal belongings, such as how many dogs or cats lived in their household, if any. I could even determine how many humans lived in their house if I had enough snooping time on my hands. I was always careful to retreat from these private areas when I heard the car coming up the driveway on their return, so my snooping went undetected as far as I knew. At least I never heard any guest complain to my family that their space had been disturbed or violated. Once I even took a nap between the sheets of the unmade bed of one of my parents' guests and almost got caught. Because I was so comfortable, I slept through the sound of the car doors slamming when they all returned. Had it not been for the sounds of the clambering of feet and laughter as they climbed the stairs from the garage when they returned home, I would have surely been caught. My fur still stands on end when I think about how close I came that day to being caught red-handed when after quickly pulling myself together just in time, I was able to greet everyone at the kitchen door. Those company weekends would eventually end, and I was always a little sad to see the people go; but their last morning with us usually meant a big breakfast, which included bacon, and that meant a bacon-grease basted Milk-Bone for me. It also meant our quiet little household routine would resume, and I'd have my parents' full attention, which was as it should be.

My Boyfriend Duke

Listen! My beloved! Look! Here he comes, leaping across the mountains, bounding over the hills.

Song of Songs 2:8 NIV

I always looked forward to summers in Vermont. That was when I enjoyed my best ever dog friendship. Before I came to live with them, my parents had already become familiar with this friendly neighborhood beggar. As this gentle giant made his morning rounds, he would come daily for his Milk-Bone handout. His name was Duke, and he was an imposingly enormous German Shepherd who looked almost regal as he ambulated up the driveway on his regular route. I recall my Dad saying that Duke almost commanded your respect by virtue of his noble stature. Although Mom and Dad would have loved it to be otherwise, he stayed no longer than the time it took to eat his biscuit before majestically trotting off down the hill to the next neighbor on the road. I could hear the fondness in their voices when they spoke about him, during my first road trip to Vermont. I looked forward to our meeting with an open mind.

My first impression of Duke, when I was still a puppy, was that he was the most handsome creature I'd ever set my eyes on, and I was immediately in awe of him. I looked forward to his daily visit. As our familiarity grew and he realized I posed no threat, being a fraction of his size at that time, we began playing Tag on a daily basis. First I'd chase him but could never catch him, then, he'd chase me and catch me almost immediately. I took great delight in our game even though my loss to him was a foregone conclusion. During mud season, the yard had yet to acquire its eventual fine carpet of grass and instead would become a field of muck from being trampled under our feet. Although I was just a puppy, I could run pretty fast, which wasn't really a challenge for the full grown Duke, but he pretended that it was a challenge to appease me. He was a kind and considerate soul of a dog. Otherwise, he probably wouldn't have given me the time of day. As I grew up and realized how he'd patronized me when I was just a pesky runt, it only served to make me admire him more. Even after I grew to my full adult weight, I was dwarfed by Duke's great massive body. I was never to be a formidable opponent for him, but we continued our chasing game regardless, just for the sheer fun of it. Always the loser, I would lie on my side panting from exhaustion while he flaunted his victory over me with his amazing, laughing eyes. Then, as suddenly as he'd appeared, he loped back down the driveway toward home, leaving me exhausted and covered from head to toe with mud.

At that time, I had no real friendships of a canine nature to speak of during all the long Massachusetts' winters. So every spring, as we prepared for our return to Vermont, I'd eagerly look forward to reestablishing the close relationship I'd forged with Duke. Then the unthinkable happened one year after we arrived back for the season. Mom and Dad were still unloading the truck, and I was allowed to stretch my legs, as was the usual custom. Not wasting any time, I headed for the front deck, which was the highest vantage point I could obtain to provide me with the best view down the long driveway. The ritual was always the same. I sat on the deck and hypnotically stared down in the direction of Duke's house. Then, using the mental telepathy skills I believed that I had, I sent a message to Duke that I was back for the summer and available if he was up for a game of Tag. The minutes ticked by, and I stared straight down the driveway for several moments, not moving a muscle. That day, as I expected, his head appeared over the crest of the hill on his stately approach. I leapt off the porch and ran to greet him in an annual reunion rite born of mutual affection and the unbreakable bond we had. Unfortunately, I was taken by surprise by the sight of what followed behind him. A small, pale-eyed mongrel sprinted in tandem with my black knight as he trotted toward me. I stopped short and could barely contain my contempt at the sight of my snake-eyed rival. As it's been pointed out on a number of occasions, I am prone to jealousy. Because of this, I impulsively instigated the first dog fight of my young life. The fight was short-lived as the other female, shocked by my unexpectedly harsh greeting, had no penchant for conflict and gave in at the first sign of provocation from me. No blood was shed, but emotions ran high that day on our hill. The short battle resulted in my earning the honorary title of alpha female in what was now a pack of three.

When the neighbors, Duke's parents, came up later that day to greet my parents on their return for the season, I learned that Duke's female companion was his newly adopted sister, Zillah. She was somewhat of a misfit and was rescued just before she was scheduled to be euthanized by the overpopulated local animal control facility. Fortunately for her, she'd caught the eyes of Duke's parents who happened to be at the shelter on that particular day in search of a winter companion for Duke. Looking back on it, she was sort of cute in her own way, and once I got to know her better, I tended not to notice her shortcomings in the beauty department. For some reason, though, humans found her appearance to be quite endearing. From that day on, she accompanied Duke on his daily biscuit rounds. I was able to fake an appearance of tolerance toward Zillah, at least for Duke's sake, and because of all the kindness he had shown me in the past. For the record, although Duke liked me better and for the sake of not hurting her feelings, he always took a neutral stance with me around Zillah. I guess he felt there was enough of him to go around.

On our return to Vermont for the season from Massachusetts, one spring day years later, Dad was having trouble getting the truck through a snow drift on the driveway, and I was whining in the back seat, champing at the bit to get out and run, so Mom and I exited the vehicle at mid-driveway. Duke wasn't around, but Zillah spotted us from our neighbor's yard and sped toward us, excited at the sight of Mom. My jealousy got the better of me, and I literally saw red when Mom bent down to pet her. It was purely an instinctive reaction when I lunged at Zillah. Mom's failed attempts to get between us only served to intensify my anger. The fight lasted for a long twenty seconds, and though the spit had flown, as usual no measurable amount of blood had been shed. Plenty of angry words were exchanged that day between me and Zillah—words that had gone unsaid for too long. As a result, our long-held truce of several years ended. After that incident, we no longer had to endure the façade of our quasi-friendship, and Zillah stopped accompanying Duke when he came over. Mom never realized this, but after that fight, I was keenly aware of the fact that she continued to be friendly toward Zillah, in spite of my misgivings; and that she even allowed Zillah to accompany her on road walks, which I was not allowed to go on, lest I try to take a road walk by myself someday. Zillah's distinct odor on Mom's hands and walking stick when she'd return was a dead giveaway, although I'm sure if I'd been able to ask Mom point-blank if it was true, she would have denied it, not out of malice but to save my feelings. Duke continued to visit almost every day, but as the years passed, he moved at a slower pace and with an obvious limp. Our racing days had become a thing of the past. That was okay with me because I was beginning to experience my own joint pain.

The time did come when Duke no longer appeared on our doorstep. That also was the year that my noble knight in shining fur armor passed away. I still think about him a lot and miss him dearly. I had been able to smell death upon him before he passed, so I'm guessing he probably knew in his heart that his days were numbered, as I know mine are now. Not understanding the finality of death at that time, I continued to wait each day for him for the rest of the summer, sending telepathic messages from the deck, but he didn't come. Eventually he just became a wonderful memory to me, and I learned to make other friends, although not with Zillah. I sometimes have suspected that Duke was the one who borrowed my deflated football that had gone missing in my youth. I took it upon myself to go snooping at his house one day after he died when his family wasn't home. I knew Duke, wherever he was, would understand. My snooping turned up nothing of my football, but I did notice Zillah watching me from their back porch, and her squinty eyes looked guilty in my opinion.

Since my end is near, I've been having a lot of nightmares. I had a dream last night that I was in a car flying down a highway. I was in the backseat, and when I sat up, I saw that Duke was driving the car, Zillah was riding shotgun, and Champ was on the hood of the car looking at us through the windshield. It freaked me out because Duke was driving all over the road while Zillah was laughing like crazy, and Champ was hanging on for dear life. My stomach was doing flip-flops, and I was barking for Duke to stop the car. I began to pant and whimper in fear when suddenly... Mom woke me up.

In the summer of my tenth year, Mom and Dad were making plans to attend a wedding in upper-state New York. Usually if they were taking a short overnight trip, I was lodged at the local animal hospital's kennels, something they were reluctant to do unless there was no other option. This particular facility didn't have very large kennels, so it made for a long absence from them for me; and although I didn't complain, it was never my preferred lodging when they went out of town. On this particular trip, they planned to be leaving on Friday and returning on Monday or Tuesday morning; and since the animal hospital wouldn't be open on Sunday, I would have only one opportunity to do my *business* when a kennel employee would arrive to release me from my kennel on Sunday afternoons. This wouldn't have been a problem as far as I was personally concerned, as I could be quite the camel if it was necessary, but Mom was stressed about it being insufficient for my needs. I was relieved when it was decided that a three-or four-night stay for me there was out of the question. I blame myself for Mom being misled about my frequent bladder urges because I often pretended I had a pressing need to *go*, so I would be allowed outside after dark. This was a time of day that the nocturnal creatures came out. For some reason, my parents feared that this posed some sort of a danger for me. I'm certain no other excuse would have worked, other than blatant faking of urinary urgency.

There was another reason they regretted leaving me at the animal hospital for boarding. On one of my stays there, I failed to relieve myself during the short time I was allowed in the area of dog runs provided for that purpose. I tended to be finicky about where I *went*, so it usually took me longer than most dogs to finally decide on the ideal area to do my *business*. My failure to *go* within the allowed time went unnoticed by the kennel staff, and I subsequently held my bladder's contents for an additional twelve hours at which time Dad picked me up. As I was impatiently waiting for him to pay the bill at the reception desk, and I was about to explode, I lost control and relieved myself of about a gallon of urine as I stood over the drain in the center of the floor of the waiting area. I was unable to stop the stream once it started, and this embarrassed Dad more than it embarrassed me. For some reason, we weren't barred from future visits to the clinic, so I'm guessing I wasn't the first dog to have done this.

So the decision was made not to send me to board at the veterinary clinic that weekend of the New York trip, and instead a call was made to Mom's friend and neighbor, Ginny. Ginny had three dogs living with her and had offered her dog-sitting services to my folks should they ever be needed in a pinch. I had only met one of the dogs, Charlotte, a mostly Yellow Lab mix who was thirteen and slowing down like me in many ways. We always got along very well as long as I let her be the boss when I was at her house. Ginny's other two dogs were actually her granddogs that had been left in her care when the kids had moved on after college to have their own places—apartments that didn't allow dogs. Since I had never met Ginny's granddogs, I was curious as to what the dynamics would be now that there were other dogs to contend with besides Charlotte. I had no negative preconceived notions and looked forward to the change in my routine. The day my parents left, I was dropped off by Mom at Ginny's house early in the morning just before Ginny was herself leaving for work. Before going, though, she took the time to introduce me to her new charges, a male Rottweiler named Attila and a female Cocker Spaniel named Goldie. I could tell right away that Attila didn't like me and neither did Goldie for that matter, but no signs of outward aggression were displayed in front of Ginny, who, feeling it would be safe to leave us alone, left for work.

The day had a rocky beginning as Goldie started in on me right away—letting me know that in the household pecking order, my place was at the bottom, and that I should watch my step if I knew what was good for me. Having made that clear, she stayed closely at Charlotte's side and stepped in between us every time I attempted to approach Charlotte in familiarity. I was disappointed because it occurred to me that my former friendship with Charlotte was a thing of the past, and now that she lived in a multi-dog household, I was strictly an outsider. In her new role as alpha dog, Charlotte wasn't her usual friendly self toward me either, and teaming up with Goldie, they shoved me around and nipped me until I squealed for them to stop. It didn't really bother me though, because we dogs instinctively understand this is only a controlled rite to establish who the leader is and then the followers. You see it all the time at dog parks and dog daycare centers; human owners often panic when they see their dogs seemingly being bullied. In fact, it's only the natural way that dogs communicate with each other and establish boundaries. Most dogs understand this, and usually there are no hard feelings, and no real pain is inflicted in this particular kind of dog hazing. It would serve humans well to understand this dog code of behavior too, so there wouldn't be hard feelings among the dog owners at those parks and daycare centers. Back at Ginny's that day, this initiation had been expected by me and was just enough to allow Charlotte and Goldie to establish rankings, but not enough to leave any marks or otherwise hurt me. By mid-morning, the sparing was over and it was clearly understood that Charlotte was the alpha female, and Goldie was next in line. I was covered in spit, but as long as I didn't override this order, we females would get along just fine.

Attila, the male Rottweiler, appeared to have the potential of being a bully and a rascal, though I couldn't prove it by anything in particular he did. I wasn't able to figure him out by scent alone, so I spent most of the time just trying to stay out of his way and hoped he would forget that I was even there. I could readily smell his aggressive nature, and my senses warned me that he could be trouble if I didn't stay on my guard. He lay sprawled out near the stairway, blocking the entire kitchen entry—a kitchen in which sat a large bowl of kibble that Ginny had generously left for us. It was meant to tide us over till dinner along with a couple of bowls of water, yet it remained unattainable to me. Attila stared at me with a mischievous twinkle in his eye for most of the morning and into the afternoon, guarding the food and water from *me,* although Charlotte and Goldie were given free passes to walk by him unchallenged.

I suspected that Attila was plotting something malicious for an initiation rite of his own, and I was getting nervous. I was also very thirsty after the earlier skirmishes with Charlotte and Goldie, and although I was usually able to come up with a solution through ingenuity and resourcefulness, that day I was drawing a blank. In my unwillingness to draw any attention from him, I remained quiet and as much as possible, out of sight, knowing well that he could smell my presence anyway, and I wasn't fooling him. Minutes then hours ticked by, and I was beginning to feel seriously dehydrated. I began inching my way toward the stairs in an attempt to get to the upstairs toilet, which I knew existed because I'd heard the flushing earlier that morning. It would involve hurdling a baby gate, which barred the household dogs from going upstairs but was no obstacle to me, a dog who had been hurdling barbed wire fences, gates, and stone walls from a standing position (and without benefit of a running start) her entire life. Finally hearing Attila begin to snore, I made my move and vaulted the baby gate, amazed that my arthritis allowed me to still be able to do this. I headed straight for the toilet and drank almost the entire contents before I felt fully replenished. While I was upstairs anyway, I inspected all the rooms; and after hollowing out a bed for myself with the pillows and blankets on top of Ginny's bed, I slept away most of what was left of the afternoon. The sound of her car door slamming woke me up hours later, and I attempted to get back to the other side of the baby gate before she got into the house, but Attila stood guard and prevented me from doing so. As was to be expected, Ginny wasn't happy about my invasion into the no-dog zone. Thinking back on that time now, I'm certain she was equally unhappy when she later found the dog fur I know for sure I must have left on her pillows—the very pillows I'd used to help build my dog mattress on her bed.

Fortunately, once Ginny was home for the evening, much of the aggression and tension cleared. When we were taken outside to do our *business*, there was a lot of marking and re-marking going on as we ran around the perimeter of the yard, every dog for herself or himself, staking claims everywhere. That over with, Ginny fed us; and the playing field was equaled, at least for the time being. The next morning, I lay on the living room carpet watching Ginny going in and out of the house to unload groceries from her car, always being careful to shut the door each time. On one trip, though, the door didn't latch, and a breeze blew it open slightly. I watched in disbelief as Charlotte used her nose to widen the opening and made her escape outside leaving the door wide open behind her. As I was looking out the open doorway, I saw her walk right past Ginny who was distracted by something and didn't notice. My first thought was that I didn't want to be left alone with Attila and Goldie, so without giving it much further thought, I bolted through the door and followed Charlotte into the back yard. I did look back and saw Ginny, apparently not aware of our escape, going back into the house and shutting the door behind her. It was clear to me, and I was so thankful too that Attila and Goldie hadn't been able to make their escape with us. Since she apparently had done this before and knew the way, Charlotte beckoned me to follow her, and we ran off into the woods that surrounded Ginny's large yard.

Glad to be alone with her and hoping to reestablish our former simpatico friendship, I was a willing captive and let her lead the way. Almost immediately, Charlotte led me on a pursuit of a group of deer that easily outran us. Following her nose and me following her, Charlotte then took us on a hike that I thoroughly enjoyed as it was more forest-like than my family's holdings of fields and apple orchards. We stopped only to drink our fill from a spring-fed stream before continuing on as she took me on what appeared to be a familiar trek for her. The air was so fresh and cool in those woods, and it was like old times when it was just me and Charlotte, two aging canines, without the messiness of personalities and class warfare, which had marred the day before. After about twenty minutes of poking around into ground holes, looking for rabbits, woodchucks, voles and mice, and disturbing the peace of the forestland, we came to a road. I watched with hesitation as Charlotte leapt over the drainage ditch and proceeded to walk down the road in her familiar limping gate. I'd never been taken on a road walk before, and since a terrible experience when I was hit by the mailman as a youngster, I always avoided walking on or crossing roads. I was unwilling to follow her, even though she barked at me ordering me to do so. Eventually, she gave up and moved on without me. Not knowing what else to do, I sat down on the forest side of the drainage ditch that she'd vaulted and whimpered nervously, hoping she'd come back, but she didn't.

After a while, I got hungry and thought about a dog biscuit with peanut butter on it but remembered that my Mom was away, and then I remembered the bowl of kibble that was always left on the kitchen floor at Ginny's. I followed our scent back to the house. The door was closed, as I expected it would be; but after hearing me bark, Ginny let me in, obviously disappointed that Charlotte wasn't with me. I knew she was frustrated with me as she tried to get me to show her where Charlotte was, but I was tired and hungry and having a hard time focusing on anything other than food. Ginny loaded me in the car and we drove up and down the roads with her calling out for Charlotte from the open window. I felt so helpless, and I assumed she blamed me for Charlotte's disappearance. After a frantic evening of hearing Ginny's phone calls in her quest to find her dog, I was left out of the search party once Ginny determined I was "no Lassie," an apparent insult that went right over my head. To my relief, the granddogs, sensing the family was in distress and that Charlotte had been placed on the missing dogs list at the local animal shelter, suspended the established rules of the pecking order, and we banded together in a show of support for our missing comrade. Expecting that we wouldn't be getting much love and attention that night from Ginny, we soldiered on. It was to be a long night, as none of us slept well with the fretting Ginny pacing the floor and calling periodically from the doorway for her favorite canine friend of thirteen years. At this point, my weekend adventure had turned into a bad joke, and I began thinking about my own parents. I wished they would come back and get me. Early the next morning, the phone rang; and soon afterward, an elated Ginny got into her car and took off, giving us no clue as to what it was about. From her improved attitude, we were left feeling hopeful and crowded together at the bowl of kibble. A few hours later, she returned with Charlotte in her arms.

Worn out and dehydrated from her adventure, Charlotte had traveled to the next town, an incredible distance for a dog, particularly an old one. I heard Ginny tell the story over and over as she made phone calls to all who'd been on alert over Charlotte's disappearance the day before. Charlotte showed up that morning on the doorstep of a farm. Fortunately for her, the farmer was a lover of dogs and had elderly dogs of his own; so after giving Charlotte plenty of water, he called the police with her dog tag number, and they were able to determine who her Mom was. After being treated for dehydration at an emergency animal clinic and released, Ginny brought her home again. Although we were excited to have Charlotte home, we were imprisoned in the kitchen where we were barred from playing with her while she recovered. Before going to bed that night, Ginny set up the baby gate at the entrance to the living room, so Charlotte (who normally slept upstairs in Ginny's room) could continue to rest and recuperate on the couch as she seemed to be still too weak from her experience to negotiate the stairs. I knew that the baby gate was no obstacle for me, and I easily could have vaulted it if I chose to do so; but out of consideration for Ginny and all I'd put her through, I decided to respect the boundary. As we dogs secretly know, we could still communicate with Charlotte verbally using low rumblings and other sounds that only we can make. In this way, we communed well into the night, long after Ginny retired up the stairs, exhausted. Some time much later, after we dogs finally fell asleep, I woke to the sound of Charlotte limping slowly up the stairs to her mom's room.

My parents arrived back from their weekend in New York the morning after Charlotte's adventure, and again I heard Ginny tell the amazing story of the marathon walk, leaving out all the fun Charlotte and I had had at the beginning of it. She never did tell them about my part in the escape. I don't think she deliberately withheld the information; she was just overwhelmed with her own joy at being reunited with her beloved pet.

Remembering Charlotte's adventure just reminded me of a dream I had about a month ago when I was still able to get around but just barely. I dreamed that I ran all the way back to Doug's old house without getting tired or sore as I ran. The strides I took in the dream were at least ten feet in length, and I was able to cover an incredible distance, at least a couple hundred miles, in a very short time. I was practically flying, and it seemed as though I was weightless, and the progress I made was effortless. I can't begin to express the incredible joy and exhilaration this pain free excursion gave me. Should there be a paradise for dogs when we die, I hope to experience this firsthand. I dreamed that when I arrived at Doug's, he was gone, but I was able to locate the toys we left behind when we departed on our Florida trip. My stick was still where I left it. After a little digging, I found the pink football and the rubber squeak bone too. I was so excited to have my toys back, and the dream seemed so real that even after Mom woke me up from what she thought was a nightmare, I still looked for those toys for days after. I could almost smell them as I searched high and low before I finally convinced myself it was a dream. I only wish my folks would let me finish my dreams sometimes!

All Creatures Great and "Tall"

God made the wild animals according to their kinds, the
livestock according to their kinds, and all the creatures
that move along the ground according to their kinds. And
God saw that it was good.

Genesis 2:25 NIV

Not all of my non-human encounters were with domesticated
animals and probably, unless they were more observant than I've
given them credit for, my folks had no knowledge of most of these
relationships. It wasn't always direct or friendly interaction either
but usually just simple observation surreptitiously conducted
from a secure outpost within viewing range of the object of my
fascination. I had to be careful to always stay downwind from
whatever creature it was. Because I'd discovered that the direct
approach with regard to feral animals was usually met with some
kind of hostile confrontation, I found the silent approach was the
best one, at least until I could gauge the risk and determine the
compatibility of our species.

I quickly learned as a puppy that insects, although interesting
to watch, were not my friends. The sting of a wasp landed quite
a punch, I found out, and wasps could be easily riled into battle.
I learned my lesson one day as I curiously placed my nose into
a wasps' tunnel in the ground. Once it became clear to me that
those strange brown projections that hung on almost every
outside corner of the house and garage were highly guarded

wasp nests, I steered clear of them but not before experiencing the wasps' angry response to an invasion by my curious snout. Bees also tended to sting, I found out, and when disturbed would swarm and force me to seek refuge. Because of this, whenever a flying insect's nest got in my way, I gave it a wide berth, especially if the nest appeared to be dormant. We found this out the hard way when late into the fall one year, Richie, Mom and Dad's grandson, was visiting, and he came in from playing in the field proudly carrying a seemingly inactive wasp nest that he planned on bringing to his next boy scout meeting when he returned home to Massachusetts. Although the nest appeared to be empty, it was found to be loaded with wasps once it was brought into the warm house.

Other flying insects, such as black flies, were mostly a nuisance for me because of the insidious nature of their bites. These didn't start itching until the deed had long been over, and so I couldn't swat them with my paw or tail in time. They were common during the spring months. Of course I'll never forget the deer flies that made a mid-summer appearance annually, torturing all of us with their fierce bite that would leave a huge welt on their victim. The deer flies were usually gone about a week or two later when the dragonflies came to our rescue and feasted on them. Grasshoppers, spiders, snakes, grubs, and beetles held no particular fascination for me as long as they didn't invade my space when I lay upon the ground. I tried to be careful, but sometimes my nose would unexpectedly penetrate a carefully crafted spider's web as I ran through the higher grasses and wild berry patches. I really didn't like the sensation and did get an occasional bite from the web's unhappy occupant.

Butterflies were plentiful on our hill in Vermont. Mom said the Monarch butterflies were prevalent because of the high volume of Milkweed that grew on our land. The delicate structure and graceful fluttering of the butterflies enchanted me. They often tried to engage me in a game of Catch Me If You Can as I rested in the grass. I was never able to catch those illusive creatures during this game. Sometimes due to my clumsiness around diminutive things, I did inadvertently damage a wing when I'd come upon a butterfly—resting on the clover and unaware of my approach, it wasn't able to escape the greeting I made with my paw.

Birds were another species that caught my attention. Over my lifetime, I've observed many varieties, but there was one kind that I feared above all others. Mom and Dad referred to them as "planes" or "jets," and they made a horrendous sound like a mighty wind, or even worse, a hurricane. The smaller ones had the most fearsome aggressive nature, and they sometimes flew menacingly over our land, causing me to hit the deck when they "buzzed us" as Dad put it. I quickly got used to it, but I was still fearful that the plane might try to nest in one of our trees; so when they flew overhead, I would bark madly in warning to chase them away. Apparently, they heeded those warnings because they never did land on our property. Neither did the giant mosquitoes Dad called "helicopters" that sometimes hovered high above our mountain ridge.

As my knowledge grew through the years, I learned to gauge the approach of warmer weather by the distinguishable chirping of the many songbirds that returned each spring. At times, a hummingbird would hover just inches from my eyes and suddenly speed away. They seemed to be attracted to the many flowers that grew around our cabin. Birds were always quickly airborne and out of my reach, so I had very little direct interaction with them—with the exception of being occasionally pecked on my head by a dive-bombing Blue Jay that felt I'd threatened her nest. The crows came each summer to inspect the freshly planted green beans and corn. I gave up trying to intimidate them as they laughingly cawed at me and boldly snatched the seed they coveted so much.

There was a beautiful black bear with cubs that held my fascination one year. They had a lair not so far from, but out of sight of, the house; and I'd crouch behind an outcropping of rocks I'd found downwind of the den to spend time observing their interaction with one another, until they'd wander off in search of food. The mother lovingly tended to the needs of her young and never allowed them to wander far from her, although they did seem to present a challenge to her as they grew. It reminded me of how much I missed my birth mom. Until I'd seen this bear mom being so protective and caring of her young, I'd never really fully appreciated my birth mom's maternal efforts. Often when the bear and her cubs would wander off, I'd stay behind, taking advantage of their absence to roll in their waste. Doing a thorough job of it, I'd cover my thick mane with bear scat, knowing that my parents would fail to appreciate why I did this. In addition to it being an instinctive safety measure, applying their scent to cover my own, thus avoiding detection, I have to admit I also found the scent intoxicating. Being given a soapy bath each day that I returned from these excursions was positively the most annoying thing my folks did to me.

It was sometime in late summer that the mother bear was alerted of my presence when I inadvertently walked upwind of her lair. Looking distressed, she rounded up her cubs and herded them off quickly until they were all out of sight. Sensing her fear and urgency to retreat without incident, I instinctively held back and chose not to follow them. I suspect that if I'd pressed the matter, she might have presented me with a formidable challenge, judging from those massive claws of hers. I waited for her to return with the cubs for what seemed like hours, long after sunset. I tried to ignore the sound of Mom and Dad's incessant calling of my name in the distance. My irritation grew as I was certain their persistent shouts were keeping the bears away, but they never did return to the den that night. I checked the den every day and waited from my secret outcropping nearby hoping the bears would return. I began to suspect that the bear had found a new secret lair to care for her young. My daily vigil proved to be an exercise in futility, and one day I resigned myself to their permanent departure. Every year since then when we get back to Vermont, I always take some time to check out the old bear den, and I can still smell the faint odor of their composted waste deep within it.

Living in the country gave me the opportunity to observe all kinds of wildlife. Being an animal that loved to run, I particularly found pleasure in chasing the deer that seemed at first to respect my territory and stay clear of our yard. However, eventually they ignored my scent and grazed every evening practically right up to our cabin's front door. I would watch them from behind the sliding glass door and was never allowed out if they were nearby. At times, I would chase them if I came upon them grazing, just for sport not out of hunger or malice. Now that I'm older, I've come to realize they were only occupying the land that had been theirs for years before we came to live there. From hearing my folks talking about it, I came to learn that the deer had to rely on their own resourcefulness to survive the many hostile forces against them. The bitterness of winter, the constant search for food, protecting their young from animal predators and themselves from determined hunters were all obstacles to their survival. It's no wonder the deer looked at me with weariness and resentment. Sometimes, though, the deer would get the better of me, and I would be the one running for my life from them. I would have probably been hoofed to death if they'd not been so afraid to follow me right up onto the deck. Mom and Dad did allow friends to hunt on our land, and since I was afraid of the sound of guns, I didn't venture far from home during the hunting season. At those times, at least for a while, the deer had a fiercer enemy to deal with than me.

Just last summer in Vermont, Dad was on the deck grilling, and we were quietly watching a doe and her fawn grazing about twenty yards away. She seemed relaxed and unconcerned at the time, I guess because Dad's presence gave her a sense of security, so she initially ignored us. I'm not sure what it was that provoked her, but she charged toward me in a sudden preemptive strike and kicked me repeatedly as I tried to defend myself. When Dad made a move toward us and yelled, she withdrew and ran off to rejoin her offspring and continued grazing. Maybe it was payback—maybe she had just determined to bide her time and wait for my eventual old age and weakness and then make her move. Whatever her motives, I'm sure the doe felt a great deal of satisfaction that day having put me in my place once and for all. Appropriately chastened, I was shaking pretty badly and terribly sore when Mom brought me into the house to examine my superficial wounds and comfort me.

A woodchuck that my parents nicknamed "Chuckie" took up residency in the stone wall that lined our driveway. Each morning, Dad would find a large hole in the wall where the woodchuck had dislodged one of the larger stones near the bottom. Along with the discarded rock was a pile of fresh soil at least two feet high. Chuckie's nocturnal tunneling seemed to irk my Dad in the beginning. Patiently, Dad would dispose of the pile of debris and reset the stone in the wall only to find his efforts repeatedly undone overnight. What started out as an annoyance, though, became routine and actually became kind of funny. We would even find Chuckie sunning himself on top of the wall during the day, and we'd watch him from the kitchen window, which gave us the best view of his sunbathing. Dad set an apple on the wall each day for Chuckie, and by evening it was gone. He only stayed for one season. Eventually, the hole in the stone wall was permanently cemented in. There came a time when another woodchuck wandered into our yard one day. Unlike Chuckie, this one had a bad attitude. When I barked at him, he aggressively challenged me, snarling with his teeth bared and his spit flying. Then he lunged unpredictably at both me and my parents who had just been minding their own business working in the yard. Concerned for my safety and Mom's, Dad retrieved his .22

caliber rifle and ended the poor thing's life. Dad said that he was probably rabid—a thing I was inoculated against annually, lest I become rabid too.

My greatest wild animal encounter by far was the bull-moose I bravely faced-off with one chilly fall day. I was shocked at first by the sheer body mass and height of the mammoth buck I believed him to be. The rack, stretching an easy five feet or more from tip to tip, appeared to be a fearsome weapon as the giant beast bent his head low and shook it menacingly in my direction. I barked my most ferocious bark—a bark that I generally saved for moments of extreme danger, and that Mom would refer to as my "atomic bark." The moose was at least ten yards away from me, yet he barely acknowledged my warnings. For certain, he must have smelled the fear I'm sure I was giving off in my scent at that moment. I couldn't help wondering what I would do if he actually did give chase. Thankfully, he had other things on his mind and slowly sashayed on by me. Shortly thereafter, he disappeared into the woods but not before my intense barking fit brought Mom and Dad to the window to see the moose for themselves. The moose sighting at our elevation was an uncommon occurrence, according to Dad, so it was the talk of our house for weeks after.

Fear

The only thing we have to fear is fear itself.
                                    —Franklin D. Roosevelt

Fear has plagued me most of my life. Clearly, the deplorable state of my humble beginning is a reasonable explanation for much of it. However, most of it was just plain unexplainable, and it really didn't take much to scare me. It still doesn't. For instance, just seeing the vacuum cleaner being taken out of the closet can trigger a negative reaction, causing me to beg to be let out, at which time I'll head for the hills. To be trapped in the house while the vacuum is operating is torture. I'll always find a place in the house as far away from this machine as possible, even if it means squeezing all sixty-five pounds of me into a thirty-pound hiding place.

I tend to be unpleasantly surprised by sudden loud noises and will often jump to attention when I hear them. This has proven to be disastrous at those times when I've been startled, and a drink has been spilled or an item knocked over if it happened to be in the way. One particular incident stands out in my mind. It happened just a few years ago. Mom and Dad were settled down in front of the television to watch the evening news, and I laid down in one of my favorite places—on the floor right in front of them. I was stretched out to almost the full length of the couch, and their legs were spanned over me like a bridge because their feet were resting on the coffee table. I think they'd forgotten I was even down there after a while. Earlier that day, Mom had turned up the phone volume to its highest setting, so she could hear it ringing while she worked in the garden. Unfortunately, she forgot to turn it back to normal when she came in later that afternoon. When the phone did ring suddenly that evening much louder than normal, it startled all of us, but my reflexes sent me jumping to attention. When Mom tried to go and quickly answer it, my body accidentally blocked her lower half as her upper half continued to be propelled forward and downward. By the time I recovered from the fright it gave me, Mom had hit the floor head first. We never really determined who was at fault but by the next morning; Mom woke up with a black eye. Dad went out the next day and bought a cordless phone for Mom to have in the garden.

I've always had an intense fear of guns and fireworks. Since Dad sometimes has target practice, I've learned to identify the distinct scent of firearms, and I avoided going with him on those days. Mom and Dad attribute this to the possibility of an earlier shooting experience I may have had early in my life. My theory is that it had to do with one of the frequent visitors whose car would always backfire at the old house where I lived as a puppy. During the hunting season, I am tortured each morning through sunset when I hear the blast of rifles echoing over the hills. But the one thing that does scare me more than any other stimulus is the dreaded thunderstorm. Even a moderate summer storm will drive me to the basement storeroom where I stay for twenty-four hours. I will have to be literally dragged outside to do my *business*. One summer, we had an unusually active storm season. My constant state of shell shock was beginning to take its toll on my parents' happiness, so I was brought to the veterinary clinic, and Mom was given a prescription for a mild tranquilizer for me. It helped, I guess; but I sensed that Mom had a similar dread of storms, and her reaction to them only reinforced my fear—just as it had been with my birth mom who transferred her phobias to me by example.

Later that same summer while Mom and I were walking around our rolling hillside and admiring how beautiful the sky looked, a band of dubious-looking black and gray clouds came roiling in suddenly against a serene blue backdrop. Unprepared for the fast approaching storm and still a good distance from home, we quickly headed in the direction of the cabin. As the wind picked up and the sky grew more ominous, we began to speed up our pace. Suddenly, a blinding bolt of lightning followed by an almost immediate clap of thunder the size of Texas had us running for our lives as we realized how vulnerable we were out in the open and a prime target of the storm's wrath. For once in her life, Mom had an almost supernatural ability to keep up with me. In our panic though, we forgot the *buddy system*, and by the time Mom reached the cabin, she realized I wasn't with her. As for me, I had the advantage of already knowing, from secret scouting expeditions I'd made, that the closest shelter was the house of a neighbor—which is exactly where I ended up. It was a property that abutted ours at the deep end of our land, but the driveway was on a different road. The humans there were as unfamiliar to me as I was to them when we eyed each other from opposite sides of their screen door. I sat on their front porch in the pouring rain and implored them to let me in using my *look* that usually brought positive results from my parents when I wanted to be let inside. I must have looked a fright as I gazed up at them with my chattering teeth and my body quaking in terror. In the end, the decision to deny me entrance was made by their dog who apparently would not allow it, so the man attempted to order me to leave with a series of half-hearted commands to "Go home." None of his orders to disburse scared me enough to leave, and I refused to remove myself from the short overhang of the porch's roof, which was my only shelter from the relentless deluge. To his credit, the man came out after the storm had passed, and the rain had ended. He looked at the tags on my collar. Until then, I'd never understood the reason for wearing the annoying tags that jingled and gave away my position often when I was stalking or hiding. Evidently, the tags gave the neighbor the code he needed to contact my parents. Within the hour, Dad pulled into the driveway and rescued me.

I was to learn later, as I've heard the story again and again over the years, that as soon as the storm had passed and it was safe to go back out, my folks scoured the hills calling my name and had even driven up and down the road looking for me and asking around. Upon their return to home base shortly after, they found a message left on the phone from the police department informing them that I had been found by our neighbor. Apparently, my trembling had alarmed the neighbor, and he feared that I might be rabid or insane or both. At least that was the reason he gave them for not giving me shelter from the storm within his house. My parents always roll their eyes up at this part of the story, as though they didn't really buy that excuse. The truth of the matter is, there's nothing scary or threatening about me whatsoever.

I was only allowed to go down our long driveway with my parents to the mailbox if I was on my leash. As we would approach the bottom, I would be tied to a tree about twenty yards short of reaching the road, and they would continue the rest of the way to the mailbox. On the return trip, they would untie my leash, and we'd head back home. I guess their reasoning was that if I didn't actually get close enough to the road, I wouldn't be interested in it and would never go down the driveway by myself. In fact, this logic only made me more curious about the road, and I did go down one day by myself to see just what was so special about it that they would withhold it from me.

It was a gorgeous day. Mom was in the garden, and Dad was mowing the lawn, so it was easy to slip away unnoticed. I stealthily slunk down the drive, taking precautions to be as quiet as possible. My excitement was mounting as I continued on beyond what was my usual limit. When I reached the main road, I decided to sit on our side and watch cars go by; but since we lived on a cul-de-sac, few cars came along. I was frankly disappointed as I'd expected more from the road experience. Just as I'd decided it would be in my best interest to head back before my absence was noticed, I saw the white mail truck approaching. I stayed on the side of the road and watched as it pulled up to our mailbox and a man put something into it. I'd seen this before but not from that vantage point. I recognized him as the same man who'd exchanged greetings with my folks in the past. At those times, if he'd noticed me waiting for them tied to the tree, he'd give them a biscuit for me. Remembering that, I was eager to greet him myself and claim my treat. I was probably just over a year old at the time and terribly naïve still. In almost every case, humans were mostly friendly to me, so I didn't hesitate to approach the truck. Clearly, the man didn't see my approach from around the front of his truck as he slowly pulled away from the box and hit me, grazing my hip. I knew I was hurt, but my immediate impulse was to run, which I did, yelping all the way up to our house with every ounce of strength I had left from the trauma. By the time I got to the house, my heart was pounding uncomfortably against the walls of my chest, and I could barely breathe. My parents were nowhere in sight, so I scooted under the deck where my bed of earth promised comfort and relief. I think I blacked out as I have no recollection of the moments that immediately followed.

Later, I heard the rest of the story as it was repeatedly told over dinner on many occasions when we had guests. What happened was that after I was hit, the mailman continued on his way, so he apparently didn't realize at the time that he'd hit me! One of our neighbors who happened to be weeding her perennials at the time of the accident witnessed the whole thing. What she couldn't tell was where exactly I went because as I sped past her toward home, I ran as the crow flies, not using the driveway. Still, she was kind enough to phone and alert Mom and Dad right away, so they'd be expecting me. Apparently, my absence was discovered shortly after I'd slipped away earlier so a frantic search for me had already begun. When I didn't turn up at the cabin right away, Mom and Dad expanded their search, going in opposite directions. They shouted my name and tried not to think of the possibility that they might find me dead. I'm really grateful that Mom was able to stop long enough to consider where I might go, given that I was both scared out of my wits and injured. This thought process led her to go back up to the cabin, where she looked under the deck crawl space and saw me in my dirt bed, bloodied, scared, and aching all over. She gently pulled me out and brought me into the house where she placed me on the couch—a destination that for any other reason would have been unlikely. When Dad returned after hearing Mom's frantic calls, he placed me in the truck and rushed me to the vet. The animal doctor determined that my wounds were not of a serious nature but that I was probably suffering from shock evidenced by my severe shaking and panting. He did expect me to make a full physical recovery, so I was sent home with the order that I should rest quietly for a few days. Regrettably for me, the mental scars of that road ordeal would stay with me for the rest of my life. It was, however, the one fear my parents were glad that I had. After that, when I went along for our mail walks, I voluntarily stayed back, untethered, to let my folks approach the mailbox without me. This episode ended my fascination with the road.

Fire is another one of my phobias. I've always dreaded the one thing my folks loved to do sometimes on cold winter nights, and that is sit in front of a blazing fireplace. An incident involving fire happened one winter while we were living in Massachusetts. Mom was *working* that year. She and Dad would disappear every morning after breakfast when he took her away to a place they called work. I was never to know where that place was located, but I was awfully glad when Dad would faithfully return Mom to me late every afternoon. Without Mom home, I was left with nothing better to do than to pace from room to room in boredom, thinking about Vermont and longing to be there. Even the plastic squeaky toys and braided rope my folks had given me for my birthday failed to hold my interest for very long, unlike my deflated football, which we always left behind in Vermont, so it wouldn't get lost in the move. The days were slow as molasses for me back then. Dad had his own place he called "work" to go to in the garage or in his basement workshop. Outside of sharing our lunch break together, I was pretty much left to entertain myself as best I could. As the sun would begin to set, Dad would once again go out in the truck and return with Mom! I was thrilled about her return! After our greeting ritual, I would rest my chin upon her feet after she removed her high heels and rested on the couch. In the meantime, Dad would light the burner under the spaghetti sauce, and we'd all enjoy its smell as it wafted through the room. Then the thing I dreaded most would break up this tranquil scene. Dad would put some logs in the fireplace and light a wad of newspaper to start the fire. I was reluctant to leave Mom's side, so I tried many times to ignore the popping sounds as the kindling began to burn. Instead, I tried to enjoy the heat that warmed the room. Most of the time, my fear overcame my desire to remain with them, and I'd retreat to the sanctuary of the back wall of our bedroom—the furthest possible refuge available to me. Huddled against that wall, I'd begin to shake. I would stay there until the offending flames died down to black embers, and I deemed it safe enough to come out and eat my supper.

One day, Dad decided to prepare for a fire in the fireplace *before* going to pick up Mom from work. That way, he'd save time; and after they returned home, he'd only need to open the flue and light the newspaper under the kindling. Apparently, he didn't think there was enough ashy debris remaining in the fireplace from the night before to bother removing it before putting in fresh logs. Unfortunately, he failed to detect that some of the old embers were still hot and while he was gone the newspaper flamed up and lit the kindling! The flue was still closed, and the house quickly filled up with smoke. I escaped to my usual bedroom wall as a full-blown fire raged in the fireplace. The nonstop shrieking of the smoke detector added to the mayhem. Fortunately, the fire had taken hold just moments before their arrival home so when they pulled up to the house, they could immediately see the smoke and flames through the sliding glass door. Both of them did a valiant job as they rushed to open all the windows and doors, Dad opened the flue, and Mom found me huddled in the bedroom safe and sound but not unscathed as another nail was driven into my fear coffin.

Grandparents, Grandchildren, and Granddogs

Family is the most important thing in the world.

—Princess Diana

Not long after my first summer in Vermont began, my Grandfather and Grandmother from Connecticut, Mom's birth parents, arrived for a visit. Granddad had been instrumental in convincing Mom and Dad to consider adopting a dog, deeming dog ownership a necessity when living out in the country. He had a lifelong love of dogs and in fact Granddad's dog Jessie, for whom I was named, had been his favorite before she died. Grandma was small in stature and walked with a cane and a distinctive limp. I sensed that her handicap would require my diligent attention and I worried incessantly when she was walking on the hilly terrain of our land in Vermont. I always walked closely by her side to protect her. My overprotectiveness where Grandma was concerned was appreciated by Granddad, and he let me serve as her temporary caregiver, so he could rest when they visited. Granddad died the year after I met him, and I was sad when I heard that he wouldn't be coming to visit anymore. But Grandma continued to come to Vermont over the years. She was an artist, and one year she painted an amazing picture of me with the mountains in the background. Dad's tractor was in the picture too. This painting hangs on the wall over the piano in Massachusetts, and every time I see it, I'm so happy that Grandma loved me that much that she included me in her artwork.

Over time, I came to understand that Richie and Sara were my parents' grandchildren, a relationship that I didn't understand in the beginning but was eventually able to figure out. They visited us in Vermont every summer for an entire week. I always looked forward to those visits because they lived in Massachusetts, and other than that vacation week, I usually only saw them in the wintertime. Whenever young children were visiting, I made it my job to watch over them. This was tiring at times, but I really didn't mind it. I did get nervous though if there was a group of three or more of them, because they tended to wander off in different directions, and I would have to try to herd them back together into a more manageable group that I could better keep track of. The children found my behavior annoying, and the grownups found it amusing. I heard my parents telling people I did it because I was part Border Collie, but I knew it was just a behavior I learned from my birth mom when she would protectively herd me and my siblings under the porch of the old house.

One year, my folk's granddog Champ accompanied the grandchildren, Richie and Sara, when they came for their Vermont week. Since I customarily had them to myself for the entire time, I was taken aback when, along with their luggage, they showed up with their family dog. Usually there was a certain degree of tension between me and Champ whenever the grandchildren were around because we competed for Sara's attention continually. In the end, I had to face the fact that she loved him more than she loved me. He had a peculiar facial expression that would annoy me, as if he was gloating. One day during that week, Sara bought a tin of bubble gum at a local tourist gift shop and was showing it to her brother, Richie, who by then was almost twelve years old. Meanwhile, Champ and I looked on in curiosity. It smelled the same as, but was packaged differently than, the conventional individually wrapped gum I was familiar with but never allowed to sample. The unusual, brightly decorated container dispensed a long rope of tightly coiled fruit-flavored gum into individual portions by pulling it out through the hole on the lid. Sara demonstrated how the cleverly designed tin worked when she showed it to my folks, who then warned her to keep it away from us dogs. But it was too late—we'd already seen it. I made it my mission that week to find the can of gum if it was the last thing I did.

I was not to be disappointed as only two days later Sara forgot and left the gum dispenser in plain sight on the floor of the guest room. I'll never forget how good it tasted, sweet and chewy, although I did have considerable trouble swallowing it. As usual, Champ refused to be part of my mischief when I offered him some and instead ran off, apparently to find Sara and rat on me. At first, Sara was inconsolable after finding the lidless can covered in saliva, badly mangled and empty. She did calm down later when reminded that she was the one at fault, and that she shouldn't have left the gum within my reach in the first place. I was relieved when Mom stood up for me that time, especially in front of Champ who, from the smirk on his big white dog face, was hoping I was going to *get it*. The gigantic wad of gum eventually worked its way through my digestive tract to the relief of Mom and Dad. As for the rest of the week, Sara and her dog Champ were the best of friends, and I was chopped liver. I moped around, feeling dejected. Even her brother Richie was disgusted with the gum caper and deferred to Champ whenever he wanted some dog time that week. Mom and Dad did their best to give me extra attention to make up for the shunning of the kids. I remained in a sorry state of self pity for what turned out to be a long and depressing week for me. Eventually, Sara would get over the loss of the many toys of hers that I ruined as a young dog. Over the years of watching each other grow and mature, we've maintained a friendly relationship, although never one as close as the one she shared with her own dog, Champ. I believe I'll always secretly be her Princess even though she tried to hide it when Champ was around. Even Champ and I eventually forgot our former hostilities. Although we never became best friends, we grew to be fond of one another in our geriatric years.

When I was still young, there came a time when Mom and Dad's son Ken adopted a new dog into his family as a companion for Champ. Poor Champ was ignored by Richie and Sara until the newness of the creature died down. Her name was Sadie. A beauty, though not a purebred, she was of Siberian descent and regal in manner. I was glad that she didn't come to Vermont because I thought for sure that Duke would choose her over me if push came to shove. I saw her periodically when we were in Massachusetts during the winter when we went to Ken's house for family occasions. At first I admired her at a distance, feeling shy and inferior. I instinctively knew that her ancestral lineage was of better quality than my own. She never held this against me, as though she just knew my lack of pedigree was something I had no control over. Sadie was a dog that believed in equal opportunity in the canine pecking order and was respected in the family dog community we belonged to. Although I was older, her imposing size and calm gentle demeanor made her the honorary alpha dog when we were together. During my two-week stay at their house in the winter, she was often the voice of reason when Champ and I were involved in a domestic dispute.

Except for the one year that Champ came with the grandchildren to Vermont, Richie was always ready to be my buddy. He had a good-hearted friendliness, and once I realized his boyish ways wouldn't hurt me, I enjoyed his rough play. My favorite game with him was Tug of War because he was strong and didn't give up so easily the way Mom did or let me win all the time, like Dad. Once I'd see Richie come outside, I'd frantically grab a stick, a rope, a Frisbee, or my deflated football in order to engage him in a game before he got too occupied in something else. During his teenage years, I adored running alongside of him when he'd ride Dad's Honda 250 motorcycle all over our property. It sometimes worried me to see him go so fast. It would almost appear at times that he actually become airborne when he hit a bump. I could tell from the look on Mom's face when he'd go off on the bike that she also worried. I sensed she was depending on me to keep an eye on him, and I always returned him safely home to his grateful grandparents.

After my unfortunate incident involving the mail truck, I became fearful of moving vehicles, although I loved running alongside Richie on the motorcycle or the yard tractor when it was pulling a utility trailer full of kids through our yard. Mom had an old golf cart she used to help her transport her garden tools back and forth. Richie often tried to get me to climb on board when he drove that golf cart through the fields and up and down the driveway. I know he felt that I was missing out by not riding shotgun like his dogs loved to do, but it was really more fun for me doing it my way. One time when we were going up and down the driveway, Richie and Dad were in the golf cart, and I was running alongside them as usual, laughing like crazy inside. I had my tongue hanging out, and I was looking up at them while they laughed back at me when I should have been watching where I was going. Dad tried to warn me but not soon enough, because I ran right into the embankment at the end of the drainage ditch that ran alongside the driveway. It didn't hurt, but it momentarily took the wind out of my sails, especially when they had a hearty laugh at my expense. My face was covered with mud. It was one of the few times in my life that I've been actually embarrassed. I sullenly followed slowly up the long drive. I remember my spirit of silly carefree foolhardiness dissolved in an instant of poor judgment and inattention. When I reached the top of the drive, Mom, having been forewarned of my incident, met me on my approach. After cleaning the muddy gravel off my face, she gave me one of her homemade raspberry ice-pops to cheer me back up. I soon forgave Dad and Richie for being the brunt of their joke that day, as I always did. Later that evening, Dad loaded the young children of a visiting neighbor into his small utility trailer and towed them with the garden tractor all over our six mowed acres. I was joyfully content as I ran alongside, ignoring the pleas of those in the wagon as they kept begging me to hop on board.

My parents have another son, Martin, who lived in the apartment upstairs in Massachusetts before he got married. When we were here during the winters, I saw him often. One day, Martin brought home a young puppy and named him Bullseye. When he was adopted by Martin, Bullseye looked as though he had the potential of growing into a full-sized black Lab mix; but as the years went by, he never grew larger than about twenty pounds in size. Being a half-pint was no handicap for Bullseye. When we played Tag, he could compete on an equal plane with me. He had a dark side though. Often, when we would start play-fighting, he'd fight dirty, and he wouldn't back off when I warned him to. Another thing bothered me, and that was when we'd chase each other, he'd cheat by taking shortcuts instead of going around things the way I did. It was easier from him to duck under obstacles than it was for me, due to my size. I don't know where he got all his energy from, but he was relentlessly active, always looking for a caper of some kind, sort of restless and sneaky. When Martin married Susan and they bought a house, they took Bullseye with them. I was relieved to have my outside play area to myself once again and to lie peacefully in the shade of my favorite tree without being tormented mercilessly by the little imp. While he lived here, we had to share the dog run area where we were tied if a walk wasn't possible. I tried to show him by example, but he refused to do his *business* along the edge of the wood and soiled the area of lawn where we were tied. Dad shoveled it out daily, but I could still smell it. With Bullseye gone, I had this area to myself once again. With the coming of the spring rains the new carpet of grass that followed was fresh and clean.

Bullseye has calmed down through the years. He's become a wise old thing, wiry, street smart, and gray-faced. He was blessed when Martin and Susan had two boys of their own—new grandchildren for Mom and Dad. Bullseye gladly accepts his role in the new household pecking order as the *lesser* child. These days, he faithfully serves as the unofficial guardian of those children. In his old age, his only missteps are the occasional jailbreaks from his yard, necessitating police involvement in a suburban neighborhood with little tolerance for nonadherence to the leash law. This has resulted in an impressive rap sheet that any dog would be proud to have as his legacy.

I haven't seen Bullseye for a few weeks now. Martin sometimes brings him when he stops by for a visit. I'm sure Bullseye smelled death on me the last time he came over, so he won't be surprised to find me gone the next time he comes…

When Martin and Susan added the two babies to our extended family, only eighteen months apart, Mom and Dad were really happy to have small grandchildren again. By that time, Richie, who now prefers to be called Rick, and Sara had grown into the young adults they are now. Susan goes to work, so twice a week, she drops the children off to stay with Mom. When they were just babies, I would squash myself into the space under the highchair as each child ate in turn. It was my favorite spot because it guaranteed the steady shower of macaroni and cheese or pretzel goldfish that would rain down on my head. What didn't end up right in front of my snout was soon hunted down lest I miss a single morsel. My reaction seemed to delight whichever baby was doing the dropping and tended to encourage more of the same, particularly when Mom wasn't looking. I discovered that the hands and faces of these tiny people were also a good source of food, and I loved licking them clean. I had to be repeatedly reminded to "back off" because Mom feared I'd suddenly bite them. I understand the basis for her fear as dogs have been known to snap at children even when the dog had no prior offenses of that nature. I myself never would have done such an unspeakable thing to those delicious children! As they became toddlers, they also became more mobile, though somewhat clumsily at first. I stayed clear of their unpredictably wobbly path as I didn't want to be inadvertently stepped upon or tripped over. At my stage of life, my arthritis is always a major concern of mine. I habitually avoid collision with small children or getting clobbered over the head with an airborne toy. I still do have brief moments of jealousy, although my parents are careful to give me lots of attention too. After the toddlers had lunch, we'd all go into the playroom and pick out a book for story time before we'd take a nap.

About a year ago, I stopped joining them when they'd go into the playroom, which is just off of our family room. The reason is because it requires stepping down about eight inches and then having to climb back out, which is too hard for me. Last week, though, just before my illness took a turn for the worst, I was watching Mom through the doorway to the playroom as she sat cross-legged on the floor working on a puzzle with the four-year-old while Susan, who'd just arrived, played with the toddler. As I continued watching, Dad went in to join the fun and sat down in one of the chairs to watch. There was so much contentment in the scene, which didn't seem right because I wasn't a part of it. Feeling sorry for myself, I suddenly felt compelled to remind Mom that *I* was her baby. Then I performed a monumental feat in spite of my physical handicap. I somehow quietly lowered myself down into the playroom, limped over, and got into Mom's lap where she sat on the floor. I could tell from her reaction that she must have known, from my effort to get to her, just how important she was to me because she hugged and kissed me and said, "I know, *you're* the baby!"

Boundaries

Two roads diverged in a wood, and I—I took the one less traveled by.

—Robert Frost, *The Road Not Taken*

Although I've come to accept that certain liberties in the house are withheld from me, I've never fully understood why. As a puppy, I fought hard for my rights. I won some battles and lost others, but I have no regrets. An early attempt by Mom and Dad to ban me from the use of the couch was never successful, and eventually, they gave up on that issue. However, doors were another weapon in their arsenal that did manage to keep me from areas of the house where I was not welcome. As I matured, the taboo areas became open to me because I was no longer a threat of destruction and chaos. I used this new liberty respectfully. Once I was free to move about our house unrestricted by doors, I quickly became disinterested in most of the areas previously closed to me. This didn't apply to my parent's bedroom, an area of access that had always been a goal of mine. It happened innocently enough. We were expecting weekend guests, and my folks were concerned that I could be a dangerous obstacle if I slept in my regular spot in the hallway as I might potentially trip a guest on their way to the bathroom during the night. It was decided that I would bunk in with my parents. Apparently, I behaved well enough that night that from that time on, I was allowed to sleep with them.

I enjoyed sleeping in what became *our* room and made it my job to announce it when it was time for the family to retire. To do this, I'd stand in front of Dad as they sat on the couch together, watching television. When I'd get his attention, I'd look at him, then turn my eyes toward the bedroom, then back to him, then back to the bedroom. I would repeat this gesture until Dad would say, "Go ahead, you can go to bed." Then I'd gladly haul my weary self to *our* bedroom, jump up onto the foot of the bed and allow myself the luxury of going to sleep there. When they'd finally come in and get in bed too, the crowding of their feet below me would eventually drive me off, and I'd lie at my second favorite spot—on the floor by Dad. That was years ago though. Nowadays, I've just gone right to our room without announcing first, and I take my place on the floor by Dad's side as I haven't been able to get on the bed for quite some time. Since I first started sharing a bedroom with them, I always woke up before them, and Dad would wake up next. When I was still physically able to climb up on the bed, he would move over and let me come up and lie next to him. We'd watch the morning news together on the television. Since I now have to watch the television from the floor, Dad hangs his arm over the side of the bed and rubs my head and ears.

The time did come when I was trusted completely, even to the point of being allowed to remain outside if I desired, untethered, if my folks had to go out for a few hours. That, of course, was just when we were in Vermont and only after I was well into my arthritic years and couldn't have ventured very far from home even if I wanted to. It just seemed a shame to Mom for me to be cooped up in the house on a beautiful day. Prior to having achieved this level of trust, I would stubbornly resist their calls to come indoors when I sensed I was about to be locked in the house for hours, so Mom and Dad could go do their errands. I know how much it must have frustrated them as I coyly eyed them from a safe distance out of their reach. But in the end, they always managed to trick me with a nonexistent treat from an outstretched hand. I never caught on to this method of entrapment even though it was employed regularly, including when I had to be taken somewhere in the car, which I hated.

I've become skilled at recognizing small clues in our daily routine that will warn me of a planned trip and whether or not I'll be included. A typical red flag will be when Dad brings the big cooler up from the basement and lays it on the kitchen floor, and Mom starts to fill it from the refrigerator. That means a long road trip. A suitcase on the bed has the same meaning. A less obvious tip-off is that their clothing is different than the usual daywear such as jeans and a T-shirt. Using these hints and other data, I'm able to determine the possible scenarios and formulate a plan of escape should it not bode well for me. Unfortunately, I'm no match for human cunning; and in the end, I go willingly wherever it is they take me. It's been much easier for them as I've aged, and I no longer put up the resistance I did in my youth.

Over my lifetime, I've learned to understand the human language; and although I can't speak, I've gotten better at making my desires known to my family. Once Mom and Dad became aware of my ability to understand, they were forced to spell out information that they desired to withhold from me. Regrettably, I never achieved the ability to decipher this strange and complex spelling code, so I've learned to compensate by depending on my instincts and clues. I've never taken offense when I've been kept out of the loop, and I assume it's been for my own good as my people have been gentle and kind to me all my life regardless of the challenge I sometimes posed. I had no cause to fear any plans they had for me then or now. Now that I'm old, my parents continue to show me love and compassion and try to make me as comfortable as possible under the circumstances. It's clear that they still worship the ground I walk on.

Physical land boundaries were always confusing to me. Stone walls and barbed wire are a common sight on our property in Vermont and in the woods behind our house in Massachusetts. Most of the walls and fences are just ancient relics built during a previous era and not the actual borders of the properties. Basically, my knowledge of our land boundaries was learned through being walked on a leash by my parents along what they deemed was the designated perimeter. My boundaries in Massachusetts are less complicated since I am usually tethered and escorted by a human who does know the areas we are allowed to traverse. Back when I could still run, if I inadvertently managed to escape off the leash (which I sometimes did), our territorial boundaries were so limited that exceeding them would require crossing a major roadway—something I never would have been willing to do. In Vermont, the rural nature of the town where we live allowed me to travel on foot far beyond the boundaries of our sixty-four acre tract without ever having to cross a road. I very rarely had the opportunity or the desire to journey very far from home since everything I really wanted or needed was there.

I remember one time I was being cared for by a friend of my parents whose name was Fred. We were at the cabin in Vermont, and Mom and Dad had gone on a quick trip to Massachusetts. This arrangement with Fred was only to spare me a seven-hour round-trip if my folks were only planning on an overnighter. It was a beautiful fall day. I had spent the entire afternoon begging Fred to open the sliding glass door off the deck and let me go out. I think he was concerned that I'd run away, so he wasn't willing to release me off the leash. He did reluctantly manage to break away from the computer long enough to take me to my waste area so that I could do my *business*, but that was about it, and he took me right back inside afterward. All day, he worked at the computer, and my whining went ignored. I was able to finally slip away when the kitchen door was carelessly left ajar by Fred, and it blew open. I ran off into the late afternoon free at last. I remember the overwhelming sense of freedom I felt after almost giving up, and I went far beyond the area where my parents would normally stop and turn back toward home. It even occurred to me that I might catch up with Mom and Dad, but that was only a fleeting thought because I had no scent to follow. In my reluctance to return to my house arrest, I pressed on. I was diligent to remember to mark my bearings, lest I get lost; and I managed to venture into previously unexplored territory, curious as to what lay on the outside of what I believed to be our land.

I must have travelled for quite a distance beyond that point, and the sun was low on the horizon. I knew darkness would be upon me soon, but by then I was focused on the scent of dogs I was picking up. As I followed this scent, I ran along what Dad had often referred to as an old logging road. The dog scent continued to grow stronger—something that always piqued my curiosity. I was forever curious about other dogs, so I felt it was worth going outside of my comfort zone and following my nose to see where it led. The logging road finally led me to a long narrow gravel drive, and the frantic barking of dogs filled the air. I remember I had a strange sensation as repressed memories surfaced like a flood in my mind. It was stuff from my infancy that I never remembered until that moment as I ran toward the sound. There were no details in the memories—just a strong sense that I'd been in that place before as the whole scene had an eerie familiarity. I could judge from the yelping that these were very young dogs, but at least one of them was an adult like me. I advanced cautiously because I sensed by the tone of the barking from the older dog that it would not be a friendly encounter. I slithered along in my best stalking posture, and stealthily approached the source of the porch light that guided me. Stopping short, I blinked uncertainly as I gazed up at the sight of an old house with a low screened porch with broken lattice skirting and four dogs tethered by short chains to it. Could this be the old house where I was born? No, I finally determined, though, not quite sure. There were too many trees, and there was a lot of grass in the front yard, which would have been unheard of at my old house. I looked for burn marks on the porch, but there were none. The smell was wrong too. But I have to admit that it very well might have been the house.

The barking, which heralded the approach of an intruder, brought my presence to the attention of a human who stood on the porch steps with a shotgun that I could clearly smell had recently been fired. He was barefooted, and his clothes were filthy and torn. I could smell the fear and aggression in his sweat from several yards away. Tearing my eyes from the man, I looked back at the dogs. They were more fearful than fierce and were obviously just obediently serving their master. I had an incredible feeling of empathy toward them. Although the barking had given me away, it had gotten dark enough that the man was unable to get a good sighting on me. I was aware of the limitations humans had and their inability to see in the dark. Banking on that, I held my ground in the hopes of establishing a rapport with the adult female once the man went back into the house. I felt that if given the chance, I could convince her of my friendly intentions and together, we could figure out an escape plan. Instead, the man raised the shotgun into the air and fired a round that scared me off.

I made it back home just minutes after that to my relief and that of the concerned Fred, the dog sitter, but I don't believe I slept a wink that night. I had every intention of returning to that old house to get a closer look when my parents returned, and I would once again be free to go outside untethered. I thought of myself as the only possible hope for those poor dogs and advocating on their behalf, I hoped to devise a means of releasing them from what I knew firsthand was not a wholesome existence. I felt powerless to do this on my own though, yet I knew I had to try something; so I thought that maybe if I could get Dad to follow me, which I actually did try to do a few days later, *he* could free the dogs. Instead, while I did manage to lure Dad toward the direction of the logging road, I was harshly called back when I overstepped the boundary of our land. Instead of following me, he turned and headed back toward our cabin. I could tell from the unusually strong tone of Dad's voice that I'd better do what he said, and I reluctantly followed him home. I suspect Dad already knew what was beyond our boundary and also felt powerless, like me, to rescue the dogs at that house. Although I accepted the fact that those poor dogs were on their own after that, I considered the possibility that they could still have a person like Doug come into their lives and rescue them one day. I hoped they wouldn't have to be almost burned at the stake first though, like I almost was. We left for the winter in Massachusetts a week later, and in the frenzy of the move, I promptly centered my thoughts on other things. It's funny, but I'd completely forgotten about those dogs or that house until now.

Vacations

Somehow I know we'll meet again. Not sure quite where and I don't know just when. You're in my heart, so until then it's time for saying goodbye.

—"Saying Goodbye," *The Muppets Take Manhattan*

Almost every year in late winter, Mom and Dad begin to make arrangements for their annual trip to Florida. Florida is that place that my friend Doug and I set out for back when I was still a young puppy. Fortunately for me, we never made it beyond Massachusetts; but because the experience of traveling with Doug was horrific for me, just the very mention of the word "Florida" sends me into a state of panic. Once it becomes clear to me that I don't have to go along with them on their trip, I'm finally able to relax. Although my folks really look forward to getting away from the winter cold (which I don't mind), I can always tell that they regret the part about leaving me behind—especially Mom. One of the main concerns that comes up every year as they begin making their vacation arrangements is figuring out who will be my caretaker during those two weeks they're away. Usually this isn't a major issue because I almost always spend the time with their son's family—Ken, Brooke, and the grandkids, Sara and Richie. Richie's been away at college for the last four years that I've gone over there. Although he now prefers to go by the name "Rick," he'll always be Richie to me.

Those Florida trips have always been kind of a vacation for me too as my folks can be a little depressing to be around when the winter blues set in. Getting away from them for a short time can give me a much needed boost. Ken's wife Brooke tends to be very upbeat no matter what season of the year it is, and I love the way she laughs, which she does often. It's a "good natured and contagious" laugh, as Mom refers to it. In past years, Ken and Brooke have both worked all day at regular jobs, and Sara and Richie would be gone most of the day at school or away at college. That left plenty of time for me, Champ, and Sadie to hang out and communicate in our own dog language. When I'd first get dropped off by Mom or Dad, we dogs would begin by reacquainting ourselves with the pecking order, and I then would take possession of what would be my territory for the week. This was usually under Sara's bed, as that didn't conflict with Sadie or Champ, who both slept on the floor in Ken and Brooke's room. After that, we settled into a peaceful sort of canine cohabitation.

Well, of course skirmishes did come up like the time we sparred wildly over a breakfast morsel that one of us suddenly discovered under the table. Ken and Brooke wondered what the melee had been all about when they came home to find the dining chairs all askew and one even tipped over. And there was Champ's deeply ingrained hostility toward me, which he usually managed to contain while I was there. Actually, I believe he showed a great deal of tolerance about having me there every year for a whole two weeks. I can't say I would have been able to do the same if the situation were reversed. The reason for this is that I'm very possessive of my people when other dogs are around. Ken must have guessed that there was tension after the dining chair incident because for the sake of keeping the peace, he began taking Champ to work with him after that and left Sadie and me by ourselves. Always well-behaved in front of people, Sadie had a fun side to her, and we had a blast when we were left alone. I remember one day we really cut loose, drank out of all the toilets, tried to break into the large plastic bin that held the dog kibble, finally tore the lid off and ate half of it, played King of the Mountain on Ken and Brooke's bed, took naps *in* that bed (right on the sheets!), and sat on every piece of furniture, including the couch and chair in the good living room. That particular room was Brooke's pride and joy and generally off limits unless they had guests. Somehow, this meant nothing to Sadie and me, even though Brooke had taken the time to place throw pillows on the furniture, erroneously believing it would be a deterrent for us.

It took about three or four of those annual Florida trips before I fully understood that my folks were not totally abandoning me, and it was only a temporary separation. The first of those vacations was the most painful for me, and but for the extra love and attention given to me by my wonderful extended family, I might have died of a broken heart. As I grew older, I became accustomed to our normal vacation routine and able to understand that those trips to the place called Florida were only temporary. Mom always made a vow when she'd kneel down to say her good-byes to me no matter where she was going. "See you later," she'd say—a phrase that was her guarantee or promise that our parting was not final.

A few years ago, Ken's family vacation conflicted with my parents' trip, so the search was on for an alternate dog sitter. I remember Mom disregarding every suggestion Dad made. He recommended employing a mobile dog walking and feeding service or boarding me at a kennel. Serious discussions went on over dinner every evening that weighed the pros and cons of every possibility Dad came up with. Even cancelling their Florida trip altogether was an option that was put on the table. Mom's pickiness was stressing Dad out. I remained hopeful that they'd figure something out because frankly, being with Mom had been a particular downer for me that winter. A new business had taken over the factory on the land abutting ours in Massachusetts. While we were walking through the property a few months before, as we always have done in the past, we were approached by a security guard patrolling the grounds who informed us that abutting neighbors were no longer welcome to utilize the grounds around the facility. Since that day, I hadn't been taken on a decent leash walk even though I begged Mom every day for one. So that winter, I figured I was up for any change of routine to break up the monotony of being snowbound and in a rut. I was also worried that they might decide to bring me along to Florida.

One day, while discussing her dilemma with a female acquaintance she ran into while shopping, the woman responded that her son Jason, a college dropout who'd been living at home for about a year, was unemployed, and she believed he would be the perfect candidate for the job of dog sitter. I heard Mom telling the whole story to Dad when she returned home. Apparently, the woman's son, Jason, needed the money; he happened to love dogs and had plenty of time to devote to my every need. According to his mom, Jason was mature for his age, extremely reliable and could even care for me at their house if Mom and Dad were interested. The icing on the cake was that Jason's parents could provide backup for him if he needed it. Mom had taken their phone number down and agreed to talk with my Dad about the offer, and if he agreed, she would bring me over to Jason's house to meet with them. Dad said it was a great idea, and I agreed with him, so Mom called and made arrangements for us all to meet Jason. Mom also wanted to inspect their home and yard. I immediately liked Jason when we met, and I believe the feeling was mutual. He seemed to be reasonably intelligent and competent, and I could tell that Dad felt the same way. Privately, though, Mom spoke to Dad about some reservations she had. They lived on a busier street than ours, and she wasn't as convinced of Jason's maturity as his Mom had been. Apparently, she was also concerned about the limited ability for Jason's parents to oversee his care of me due to the fact that they were both busy professionals with long commutes. Because of the nature of their jobs, they often had to work late too. As was often the case, Mom's fears where I was concerned were off-handedly disregarded by Dad and me. She finally gave in to Dad's reasoned arguments and before we left for home, it was decided that I would spend their vacation at Jason's house. The date was set, the money was paid; and a couple of weeks later, I was dropped off at Jason's parents' house the evening before my parents departed for Florida.

Mom and Dad would never fully know the truth about what transpired during the two weeks that followed. I've had to keep the secret inside all these years, frustrated in my inability to tell them myself. I know they'd be upset for sure if they knew the truth. I guess what they don't know won't hurt them. For the first week or so at Jason's, I was happy and content in a crazy sort of way. Something about him reminded me of Doug. This is weird because he really wasn't anything like Doug. Jason was more of an extrovert and party animal. After his parents would leave in the morning, within hours the house would be transformed into a hangout for all his friends. There were no rules at Jason's, and I quickly slipped back into the bad habits of my early youth. All his friends seemed to like me, and they shared their fast food that seemed to be replenished throughout the day as young men came and went. The delicious scraps that were always carelessly tossed about in the family room or Jason's bedroom became my main source of nutrition.

After a few days of this junk food diet, my bowl full of canned dog food on the kitchen floor remained untouched, dried and formed a crust of its own. As long as my food remained in the bowl uneaten, Jason neglected to open any more cans, as he concluded that I probably wasn't hungry yet. He didn't even bother to throw away the food in the bowl after it began to draw flies the size of hummingbirds. My dry kibble remained untouched also. Eventually, I was fully acquainted with a taste for junk food. I felt as though I was in some kind of time warp, and I started to think about Doug again, which is something I hadn't done in years. Although Jason's parents promised Mom they would oversee Jason's care of me, something told me they weren't holding up their end of the bargain. My uneaten dog food sat on the kitchen floor for the entire week, turning crustier and darker with each passing day. It was covered with flies and even by my standards was beginning to stink, yet his folks never said a word about it. In the meantime, I was having the time of my life, breaking every rule my parents had taught me over the years. Because Jason's friends paraded in and out of the house all day and evening long, the door was carelessly left ajar most of the time, and I was free to slip in and out to do my *business* at will. I don't believe I saw the end of a leash for the entire first week I was there, in spite of Mom's specific instruction that Jason always keep me on a leash outside of the house with "…no exceptions whatsoever!" in case I would wander off and get hit by a car. Probably because of my dietary changes, I did have a couple of accidents; but neither Jason nor his parents mentioned them and to my disgust, I noticed they often remained untouched and ignored for a long time. My water source was the toilet, and its ice cold water was always available thanks to the consideration of Jason and his friends who left the lid up for me.

Things were going along incredibly well, I thought. I even managed to tune out any thoughts of Mom and Dad, which was unusual for me when they were away. I don't know how I was able to be so fickle, but I became quite attached to Jason, and I think I would have followed him anywhere—which I did one day when he was going into town. I must have lost my mind for a moment because I followed him into the garage and hopped into the passenger's seat beside him when he opened the door. I have no explanation for my temporary insanity as doing this voluntarily, without putting up a fight, was an unthinkable act on my part. My action that day seemed to be okay with Jason, although I clearly remembered he'd been told by Mom that I was "…never, ever…!" to be taken out in the car. Although boarding that car seemed like a good idea at the time, I was going to learn a hard lesson that day.

For some weird reason, and this has never happened again, I was completely at ease sitting beside Jason. I hadn't ridden in the front seat of a car since my trip with Doug, but this time seemed different. For one thing, Jason's car ran smoothly, and he didn't turn on the heat because I remember it was an unusually warm day for late winter, so he left the windows open. We made several stops to visit friends of his. I was free to get in and out of the car untethered whenever we stopped. I was mostly ignored while Jason and his friends hung out, drank beer on the porches, or went into the house to drink, sometimes inviting me in too. If I wasn't let in though, I didn't have to wait long before he eventually came back out of the house he was visiting, and I'd jump right back in the car alongside of him. All the aimless gallivanting Jason did that day is sort of a blur to me now, but I clearly remember our last stop of the day. It was late afternoon when Jason pulled into a parking space along the town's main street, leaving the window open for me.

He said he'd be right back, and I had no reason to doubt his word. The minutes ticked by, and I made a game of watching the cars go by, counting to see how many red ones there were, then I'd get bored and count the silver ones. Actually, my counting skills were extremely limited, so I mostly just looked for certain colored cars. I couldn't stop yawning and wishing Jason would come out. I was beginning to get thirsty too. When I'd gone into the bathroom at the last house I was allowed into, the lid had been left down, so I couldn't get a drink. Although it was early March and the days were getting warmer, there was still snow in dirty piles along the storm drains, left by the plows. The sun beat upon me as it slowly made its descent in the western sky causing its rays to stream through the car with full force. I began to pant— my body's attempt to cool me. My patience seriously tested, I decided to jump out and wait for him on the pavement but in the shade against the building, as I couldn't bear the sickening vinyl smell of the car seat in the sun's rays any longer. I was able to drink a little from a puddle left by some dirty melted snow, but it tasted salty.

That's where I was when the bus pulled up to a stop across the street. I watched as the people got off, and that's when I saw him. It was Doug! I only saw the back of him, but he was tall, thin, and had Doug's black unruly hair pulled back in a pony tail, and he wore a backpack. In my excitement, I ran across the busy street, causing cars to blow their horns at me and nearly got hit a few times. I made my way to the bus stop, but by the time I managed to get there, the people had disbursed in different directions, and there was no sign of Doug. Trying to find his scent, which I'd never forgotten, I wandered in and out of alleys and found my way to a large municipal parking lot behind the stores where suddenly I spotted Doug again. I ran like crazy toward him, barking my head off in my excitement. As I ran I barked, "Doug! Doug!"

I couldn't believe it when he pretended not to recognize me or my voice and ran away from me instead as if he was being chased. I finally reached him, and with my front paws landing squarely on his back, I threw my full weight against him, which broke my momentum and pushed him into a gigantic pile of plowed dirty snow. When he turned to me in shock, I looked at him full in the face and realized he wasn't Doug after all! His scent was completely wrong too, something I should have noticed during the chase; but at the time, my heart was doing the leading, not my nose.

My spirit sank so low in the moments that followed. I was amazed that after so many years and after all Mom, Dad, and I meant to each other, I still could have such a devotion to an individual who'd only been mine for a short time and had given me the slip years ago. When I think about it now, I'm shocked that I'd been so quick to run after my old deadbeat dad, someone whom I thought I'd long forgotten and whose commitment hadn't been genuine enough to last more than a mere three weeks. One good thing that came out of the excitement of the chase was that it had cleared my head, and I was jarred out of my Jason-induced trance, finally seeing him for the deadbeat he really was. At that moment, my one wish was to have my life back to normal, with Mom and Dad by my side.

Afterward, the Doug imposter continued on his way but kept looking over his shoulder to make sure I wouldn't continue the chase. I suddenly realized that if I was to ever see my folks again, I first had to get back to Jason, yet I was totally lost. I'd taken so many turns and run so far that I was disoriented and had difficulty picking up my scent in order to retrace my steps and return to Jason and his car. I managed to find the general vicinity of the bus stop, but then there was a busy street that had to be crossed—an endeavor that was a monumental task for the road-a-phobic that I was. The sheer volume of cars parallel parked along the main street increased my inability to even recognize Jason's car, which I had never taken a really good look at in the first place. Unlike Doug's wreck, which had a personality of its own, Jason's was newer and looked like all the other cars parked along the street. I was beginning to feel exhausted, and the pads of my paws stung from the salt and sand liberally sprinkled on the sidewalk's pavement. I returned to the general area I believed I'd been before I'd taken off, and I was even able to locate the building that we'd been parked in front of; but in my attempt to reconstruct exactly where I had been sitting in Jason's car, I found that another car with sealed windows was in my way. I was hot and panting, so I returned to the site against the building where I'd cooled off earlier. I remember it was getting dusky as I waited, hoping Jason would rescue me but not feeling very confident about the possibility.

I didn't realize it at the time, but I was to later find out that Jason had been in a local Main Street tavern that afternoon; and after a day of continuous drinking, he'd apparently completely forgotten about me waiting for him in the car. How else could he have done such an unspeakable thing? I've since deemed him to be of very low character, but I give Jason the benefit of the doubt and have concluded that it was not a deliberate abandonment of me. When he left the tavern shortly after I ran off, he simply forgot that he'd taken me along that day and drove home drunk before going directly to bed with at least a six pack or more of beer in his gut. (Probably more, but I heard his mom tell his dad he admitted to only a few.) I spent the rest of the day lost, sad, and wishing Mom or Dad would find me, like they always had in the past if I was lost. I knew though that they had no way of knowing I was missing while at that Florida place, and my only hope rested in Jason or his parents. At that moment, I considered myself to be intellectually superior to Jason and maybe even his parents too, which wasn't saying much. With that in mind, I resigned myself to the fact that rescue was probably not imminent. I was getting hungrier by the minute, and I remembered spotting several dumpsters located behind the stores earlier when I'd chased the Doug impersonator.

One of the dumpsters in particular smelled like the Chinese takeout Mom and Dad liked to get sometimes. Usually they didn't give me any of those leftovers as they believed I would be unable to easily digest this strange but delicious-smelling food. This fact only served to intensify my desire to try some, so that's why I picked that particular dumpster. I easily crossed the road, the rush hour traffic having long subsided. I was able to climb some boxes stacked haphazardly beside the dumpster, which allowed me to dive in. The smorgasbord available to me within the massive container would have been beyond my wildest dreams under the right circumstances. It turned out that my eyes were bigger than my stomach, and I ate an uncharacteristically light supper, avoided the spicier selections, and opted instead for portions I was most familiar with—pork fried rice and a half-eaten egg roll with lipstick prints on it. These were things I was familiar with—having secretly stolen some from the trash one time without my parents' knowledge. I took a mental inventory of what I didn't have room for, in case I would have to return again in the event of Jason's probable failure to rescue me. I was incredibly thirsty. I could smell and hear the brook that ran behind the parking lot. I was able to drink my fill after finding my way across the thin ice on the surface to a spring. The sun was setting, and the temperature was approaching a more seasonal coolness. My prospects for a place to bed down on that cold early March night weren't good. I found a quiet spot in a covered alley, which seemed to be some sort of a breezeway that linked the parking lot to the store fronts along the main street. There I hunkered down for the night, sheltered, so I thought, from the gusts that were picking up. I didn't get much sleep because the alley turned out to be a virtual wind tunnel.

By morning, my joints were aching badly from having to form myself into a canine pretzel in an attempt to preserve the little body warmth I still had. This was probably the year my arthritis pain began being a serious problem for me. Hungry again, I limped along on my frozen and stinging paw pads down the quiet Main Street sidewalk and headed toward the dumpster I had raided the night before. That's when I was picked up by the local animal control officer. I was able to ascertain the basic story of what happened from things I overheard as Jason's parents argued about it over the course of the following week. Apparently, on the morning that I was picked up by the officer, Jason's parents had come to realize that I'd been gone all night. They managed to pull Jason out of his hangover, enough to establish that he'd last seen me on Main Street the day before. With what little information they had to go on, they called the police to report me missing. Jason's dad arrived at the station to get me shortly after I was picked up, and I was kept under the strict surveillance of his parents for the remaining week until my folks came home. I only saw Jason one more time right after my rescue, and even then he had the gall to shun me. He showed no relief that I'd been found after he'd lost me, and even when I tried to show him some friendship and forgiveness, he didn't seem interested. I had a sense that he blamed me for his parents' haranguing him for failing yet again to accept some responsibility and complete a job he'd been hired to do. Or maybe he was too embarrassed to look me in the eye because he knew I'd heard his Mom tell mine he was mature for his age.

I saw more of Jason's parents during that final week than the previous one. They saw to it that I was fed a strict diet of my dog food with no exceptions. I sensed the tension in the household, so I withheld what would be my normal sad eye begging as I knew it wouldn't get me anywhere. I missed the junk food that once passed freely through the house every day, and I couldn't help but remember with longing the Chinese restaurant dumpster and its inventory, which I had taken a few days before. As for those friends, I saw none of them for the remainder of my time there; and I guessed, from his absence, that Jason was probably given the boot by his folks soon after my adventure, for his slovenly ways. Under the watchful eyes of Jason's dad, I was reacquainted with my leash and diligently taken out for my *constitutional* twice a day. His folks weren't as much fun as Jason, but under their management, the blisters on my feet healed, and I was restored to full digestive health and regularity by the time Mom and Dad returned from Florida. They were never told by Jason's folks what had happened during my stay there. A couple of vacations later, I cringed when I overheard Mom inquiring as to the availability of Jason's dog sitting services in a call she made to his mom. She was told that Jason was off attending college and unavailable. I breathed a sigh of relief when I heard Mom tell this to Dad.

Through Thick and Thin

If having a soul means being able to feel love and loyalty and gratitude, then animals are better off than a lot of humans.

—James Herriot

During our lives together, health issues were sometimes an inconvenience and a nuisance. There's nothing that tests faithfulness and loyalty more than how the illness of a loved one is dealt with. In the relationship between a pet and its owners, the resolve to weather the storms of sickness with compassion and caring, through thick and thin, necessitates true commitment. Putting that loved one's needs over self-interest is a measure of true devotion and sacrifice. I know that Mom appreciates all the times that I lay upon her bed holding vigil by her side when she's had one of her many migraine headaches or other sickness.

Those can be long boring days for me, but I worry about her when she's not herself. In some ways, I feel like I'm the mother for a little while, and she's my primary concern. At those times, I just couldn't go out and have any fun knowing she's unwell and indisposed. My place is there with her just in case she needs me. I never cared how positively awful she looks while having a migraine. She'll lie against the pillow with her arms over her eyes, in a fetal position. If it's a really bad attack, her hair will be all askew because she won't bother to brush it and her face gets pale and damp. Sometimes if she's weak enough, she won't even get up to brush her teeth, so her breath might be kind of awful too. The expression on her face during those headaches is difficult for me to look at because I can almost feel the pain she's going through. It's not a pretty picture, but I love her just the same.

We dogs don't care whether or not you've showered, put on makeup, brushed your teeth, fixed your hair, or are going bald. We don't care if you're schlepping around in an old pair of sweats, wearing an oversized worn T-shirt, and filthy slippers. A dog will care when things are emotionally *off* with her people or if the people seem physically unwell. Often we are even aware of these problems before the human begins to exhibit manifestations of their illnesses, and at times, we've even had the responsibility of alerting our humans to their own health crisis. You can't lie to a dog and tell us that nothing is the matter. We already know the truth long before you're symptomatic. I've known firsthand the discomfort of sickness, and my ability to sympathize helps me be a better caregiver and comforter. At least that's what I heard Mom tell Dad one time when he attempted to shoo me out of the bedroom, so she could rest, but she insisted that I stay.

It would make perfect sense for humans who suffer from various ailments to get a dog. Mom says dogs have been known to lower the blood pressure of those who suffer from hypertension. I'm not sure what hypertension means but I'm sure she's right. Dad used to have hypertension but doesn't anymore. Individuals who might be overweight for various reasons can benefit from having to walk us every day as that provides them with regular exercise. Our antics have been known to draw out those who are suffering from clinical depression. Humans who have lost loved ones are certainly helped by our devoted companionship. Most of us adore children and have exhibited extreme tolerance to their occasional misbehavior. Some of us can even stand up to the abuse that comes with having our ears and tails playfully pulled or being ridden upon as if we were ponies by small children. Usually we shy away from children if we instinctively deem them to be too rough in behavior or if they show signs of fear at our approach. We have even been shining examples to mischievous children on the value of being good and the rewards it brings. Our ability to be nonjudgmental and unbiased makes us an excellent companion choice for socially challenged individuals—as was the case with Doug. Best of all, we've been the animal of choice for serving those humans who have physical disabilities.

As a companion, we're only too happy to listen to our humans rant or complain about their problems. We're good listeners, and although we're unable to offer much insight or solve a human issue, we will *never ever* betray a secret that a human has entrusted us with! Any bad habits or behaviors that we observe going on behind closed doors will be taken with us to the grave. Whatever that odd behavior is, we will adore our people regardless. When we are sometimes inadvertently caught in the middle of a human's bad mood, an argument, or if we get yelled at for something we didn't do, we are quick to forget the injustice, and our humans are forgiven without question.

Another thing about dogs is that it really takes a lot to disgust us, and smells generally don't bother us either unless they are a sign of danger. Because of this, we're comfortable living in a house that's as neat as a pin or one of chaotic disorder. Humans don't have to keep the house dusted and swept in order to impress a dog. It is true that we don't care to live in *our own* waste, so it is still important that we are given the opportunity to go outside to do our *business*—and that should be on a fairly regular basis! Mom told Dad once about a woman she knew who would forget to take the dog out and then get mad when the dog had an accident in the house. If humans only thought about how uncomfortable it feels to have to *hold it* for a long time, they'd be more considerate about giving their dog plenty of outside time. I also heard Mom recalling a time when they visited a family for dinner, and long after the dishes were cleared away, the family's children continued arguing for an hour over whose turn it was to feed the dog. Mom said she couldn't hold her peace and finally spoke up on the dog's behalf. I almost cried when I heard that!

Hero

Heaven goes by favor. If it went by merit, you would stay out and your dog would go in.

—Mark Twain

Since my arthritis has been a problem during the last three years or so, I now tend to stay closer to home when we're in Vermont. Two years ago, I had the opportunity to prove myself a true hero for the first time in my life. It was a windy fall day. Mom had been after Dad that entire summer season to hire someone to come and cut down a tree that sat along our half mile long driveway. The tree was almost fifty feet in height and the trunk was about three feet in diameter at its base. It had been dead for many years. Its gigantic limbs loomed menacingly over what would otherwise be a lovely country lane. Often, while driving down the drive, they would encounter a freshly fallen dead limb stretched across the way, and it would have to be dragged to the side of the driveway in order for the car to pass through. Mom believed it was a matter of time before one of those dead limbs fell upon one of them. On this particular day, Mom was away visiting her family and wasn't expected home until the next day. When I saw Dad heading down the drive on his tractor with his chainsaw and step ladder on board, I sensed trouble. It's weird how dogs can tell when something doesn't bode well.

The constraints of my senior onset arthritis meant that I seldom attempted to navigate downhill especially if it meant walking back up that same hill. Therefore I stayed behind and watched Dad from the top of the drive as the tractor stopped beside the dead tree, just barely still within my sight. The breeze was pretty strong that day, and I don't know why Dad failed to take that into consideration. I can only conclude that he wanted to get the job done before Mom got back and insisted that he "hire" someone. My Dad is strictly a do-it-your-selfer and hiring an outsider to do the job would have been an outrageous concept to him. This has often been a sticking point whenever a large household project needs addressing. I watched for an hour or so as he balanced on the highest rung of the ladder to cut the limbs that were within reach and then placed them into the bucket of the tractor. That's when I suddenly noticed the large limb just barely attached to the trunk near the top of the dead tree. It was swinging dangerously in the wind as it balanced precariously on a tangled mass of other dead limbs just below it. I jumped to my feet and began limping down the drive toward Dad, barking my head off.

He didn't hear me at first because of the chain saw, but when he finally did notice me, he set the chainsaw down and began to walk up the hill toward me. Knowing that I would have been loath to walk down the drive without a serious purpose, Dad knew something was wrong. He couldn't have walked more than twenty feet toward me when we both heard the loud crack as the tree limb plummeted toward the ground and struck the bucket of Dad's tractor, sending wood flying in all directions—including right where Dad had just been standing!

After clearing away the debris, Dad drove off in his truck and returned soon after. That night at supper, instead of my usual canned food, I was given an entire family-sized sirloin steak served on one of Mom's best dinner plates, grilled medium rare and conveniently cut into bite sized pieces! A week later, a professional tree removal crew arrived with a cherry picker and removed what remained of the dead tree.

Letting Go

All his life he tried to be a good person. Many times, however, he failed. For after all, he was only human. He wasn't a dog.

—Charles M. Schulz

I can see that they're worried as Mom sits on the floor beside me and Dad sits on a chair nearby, as he is unable to sit easily on the floor because of his bad hip. The past few days were tough on all of us, and as hard as I've tried, I just can't make my legs work anymore. My hearing is poor, and my vision is a bit dulled too. I have pain in my stomach that won't quit, and for once in my life, I have no appetite, although I seem to have an insatiable thirst. Thankfully, my water bowl is kept close by my snout, and I'm able to lift my head enough to drink whenever I want to. Mom placed a couple of small pieces of the leftover Christmas ham, my favorite meat, in front of my nose; but to my surprise, it had no appeal. I didn't touch it. I can smell it though, and strangely, it's taking me back to that sweet Easter Sunday of 1992 at Ken and Brooke's when my *forever* life began with Mom and Dad.

I made a mess on the floor last night. Not wanting to soil the carpet on which I lay, I managed to drag myself onto the linoleum floor of the kitchen. Mom was so kind and understanding when she discovered it later during the night. She tearfully told me she was sorry for having slept through my need to get outside. I knew this would have been an impossible task for her to do alone anyway, which is why I never did try to wake her in the first place. As it is, between the two of them, they can barely lift me down the ramp. She cleaned up the mess without as much as a word about it to Dad this morning when he came out. It disgusted me though, to think that I'm the dog who never did my *business* on the mowed part of the lawn. I even expected visiting dogs to show the same courtesy, yet most didn't. Now I'm reduced to *going* in the house because I can't even get outside! Having to be lifted by Mom and Dad in and out of the house is humbling enough, and I almost cannot bear the indignity, although I know there is no other choice. I appreciate that they're more than willing to help me.

I've often heard them discussing how they would proceed when the end of my life came. Now that it's become a reality, they're finding it hard to let me go. I know they feel guilty too. If only I could speak, I would assure them that I'm ready to die and release them of the burden of making the decision on my behalf—just in case they later regret that decision and try to blame themselves. They had agreed, a long time ago, that should the time come when my life would cease to have any quality, along with chronic pain, they would do the merciful thing and call the vet to help me to die. I believe they're hoping this is just a temporary illness, which explains their reluctance to proceed with the plan. They also realize that they might be in denial too about any possibility of my recovering. Wishful thinking isn't what I want to hear at this time. I am, after all, fifteen years old, and this has been a slow process of diminishing health. It's time to let me go!

I'm lying here, and Mom and I gaze into each other's eyes. It's early morning, and the sun is just coming up. Once again, she spent the night right by my side. Dad has pretty much made his decision, and he's just giving Mom the time and space to come to the same conclusion. I can see that making the call is a difficult and painful thing for her to do. I haven't had much to drink since they carried me back in from my *constitutional* late last night. I can barely lift my head up to my water bowl anyway, and my wicked thirst has finally abated. We all believe that the end is closer than ever. I even heard Mom praying last night—actually, begging God to take the burden from her and take me peacefully in my sleep. I've been hoping for the same thing, and I think we probably went to sleep both feeling certain her prayer would be answered. We were surprised then, when I didn't die and woke up again to another day, still breathing, although my breaths are quite shallow. I guess God wants her to go through this experience that she dreads, and that maybe by doing so, it will give her some measure of closure. I can't convey this to her, and her tears leave me feeling so helpless. I shut my eyes, hoping for sleep to come, and try to escape the emotional strain this is putting on all of us. I know Mom will still be sitting here on the floor beside me when I wake, *if I wake...*

It was comforting to have Mom sleeping on the couch again last night just within reach of me. Sometimes when I opened my eyes, I'd find her watching me as if she was desperately trying to memorize every part of me. I know she probably didn't get much rest though, for all her crying. I don't know how much more I can take of all the stress and worry *she's* causing *me.*

It's been about four days since my ordeal began, and although I've been resolute about not being afraid to die, I've had a slight change of heart. I think it's just my fear impulse getting the better of me. I've begun to shudder too, and when it happens, I can't control it. Even Mom's comforting words and touches fail to reassure me. If only there was something on the other side of life that I could cling to or set my sights on to guide me over the hurdle. Sometimes when I try to imagine what I might expect to find there, I come up blank; and frankly, it's beginning to scare me. This must be the giant leap of faith I've often heard about but never understood the meaning of. I can see from the look on Mom's face that another long day of indecision will likely follow no doubt...

Last night, I had a vivid dream. I was running up the driveway in Vermont. At least I thought it was Vermont at first, but it was more beautiful than I even remembered it. Actually, it was more of a wooded path than our gravel driveway. There was sort of a luminescence in the air, and it was purer and fresher than ever, yet its crispness didn't sting my sinuses. There were no weeds or dead undergrowth either. All plant life seemed to be teeming with vigor, and I saw flowers larger and far more vivid in color than normal. In fact, they were colors I'd never even seen in my entire life. Oddly, I didn't have pain anywhere in my body. Freedom from pain is something I've not experienced in several years. My ability to run far exceeded what it had ever been during my lifetime and the hang-time as I ran was far beyond what I had ever hoped for. The amazing thing was that when I reached the crest of the hill, I looked down over a beautiful vista covered with dogs of all kinds at play.

A figure of a human walked among them laughing and smiling down upon the dogs and throwing balls for them as fast as one of his attendants could provide him with them. The dogs seemed to respond in joy as they ran to catch the projectiles, and yet there was a certain obeisance in their manner as he engaged them in play. The figure was adorned in regal appearing garments of shining white that gave off an intense aura of light, but it didn't hurt my eyes to look at him. His entourage of attendants—not human in form yet beautiful to look at—seemed to be enjoying his sport with the dogs, and some of them joined him also throwing the balls. I suddenly noticed one of the nonhuman beings was sitting on a stone near me, watching me. I asked him who the man was that was playing with the dogs. He told me the man was the Son of God, and that he was the king of this place I was now in, although it was just a very small part of his realm. I attempted to run down to join the group below, but I was abruptly caught up into the arms of this wonderful warm being—an angel I think—who flew with me to the most beautiful meadow, with a spring-fed stream and a pond of sparkling water. I was set down gently on a bed of sweet-smelling lush grass and told to wait. Obediently, I sat.

I didn't feel constrained by the command, just perfectly content to inhale the deliciousness of the atmosphere and see the beauty that surrounded me in that holding area where the angel had set me down. I had no fear, just a strong, strange sense of anticipation that for some reason swept over me. Hearing a yelping bark from behind, I turned around, and there before me stood my birth mom. She was as beautiful as I remembered her to be, and I was delighted to see her look so happy. In my memories, she had always looked so troubled; and of course the last time I'd seen her, she was in anguish as she looked at me from the bed of the truck as it drove away, fifteen years before. She leapt toward me in excitement, and I noted that her smell, which I never forgot, was the same. We both cried with joy as we reunited. Though we couldn't speak, we were fully able to communicate; and she told me she had come to live in this place, years before. She offered no further explanation, and I had no desire to know more. The present was enough to satisfy me. There were some other dogs with her that looked a lot like me, and I felt a strong sense of identification with them. A couple of them were still puppies, but the other three were fully grown, though not graying like me. I suddenly realized they were some of my siblings and was so relieved that they were okay, after years of worrying about their fate.

That wasn't the best surprise though. I was mistaken if I thought my joy could not be greater at that moment. A large white figure with a pink nose and a familiar twinkle in his eye was speeding toward me, barking his head off, and I almost started crying at the sight of Champ, my longtime nemesis and later, geriatric best friend. Suddenly, something in my peripheral vision caught my interest, and I turned my head to a spot on the horizon where I saw a dark figure with pointy ears running toward me. As the figure drew near, I realized it was Duke! My heart almost leapt out of my chest at the sight of him, and I ran to join him. Just as we were about to reach one another, I woke up.

Although I was initially disappointed to have had the dream end so abruptly, I believe what I had was a vision from God to calm and reassure me until my time comes to go. I noticed that my shuddering has stopped, and I've had no fear whatsoever since the dream.

My big day has finally come. After my dream last night, I'm anxious to get this process started. Mom and Dad are ready to go forward with our plan. Dr. King, my veterinarian, is away on a trip, so Dad's gone out to the veterinary clinic to see if the vet on call will be willing to make a house call. In the meantime, I rest in contentment, knowing the plan has been put into motion. I must have slept because I woke to the sound of Dad telling Mom that the vet won't make house calls for euthanizing dogs, and Mom is telling Dad that putting me in the car is out of the question. Dad was able to get the number of a traveling veterinarian who will make a house call. He makes the phone call, and he's told she can be here later this morning. This will make their long held resolve to allow me to die at home possible. Now that I know the plan is in effect, waiting for the vet's arrival is somehow bearable for me, although I can see it's still a tough struggle for my parents. My waking moments are surreal, and if it weren't for this unbearable pain every time I even take a breath, I would probably be able to wait it out and die naturally; but that may take days or even weeks, and my folks' strength is rapidly diminishing.

I must have dozed off because a car door slamming wakes me up. The traveling vet has arrived, and she's a young woman with a female assistant. I don't know exactly what it is about them, but they seem to have an odd glow about them, like some kind of an aura. It's really weird that one of them looks an awful lot like the angel from last night's dream, although she is much more human in nature. Mom and Dad are reacting normally, so I think maybe only I can see this strange phenomenon. They smile as they lean over me, and I immediately feel a sort of love or connection to them. I may have thought I would have preferred Dr. King to do this if only I could have held on, but actually, I'm glad these two are here instead. They're speaking to Mom right now in a soft, kindly whisper, as if they don't want me to overhear. I can read lips though, as I've been doing so since I began growing quite deaf during this past year. I can feel that one of them, the assistant I believe, is shaving an area on my leg. Now I can feel the prick of a needle. She's telling Mom this first shot is just to help me relax. Seriously? Mom's the one who needed *that* shot. But I let this assistant do what she feels she must, especially if it will help lessen Mom's worry. My pain seems to be subsiding a bit, and the vet is feeling around in the area of my belly. She reports feeling a hard lump there, probably the source of my pain. My peripheral vision is getting darker, and it's as if I'm looking through a keyhole or a long tunnel. I'm feeling warm too, but it's a pleasant sort of warm—like when I had my first bath at Ken's house many years ago. I'm as weak as a newborn puppy, but I'm strangely relaxed, more than I've been in a very long time. I feel so good that I wish I could tell them. I'm able to look up and see Dad watching us. He's trying to remain stoic, but clearly, he's emotionally touched by all this. I hear the vet asking my parents if they're ready. If only I could convey to them how unafraid I am, so I could see them smile just one more time. Mom holds my head in her lap and nods. Crying softly and putting her mouth close to my ear, she says those words that have always gotten me through our separations in the past, "See you later."